Praise for
BLEEDING EARTH

*STARRED REVIEW "Ward's apocalyptic novel will have readers checking the ground beneath their feet after each turn of the page. . . . Grisly and sickening (but in the best way possible), the novel more than delivers on its promise of the macabre for lovers of horror, and curious readers will close the book with countless questions about religion, science, and human nature." —*Kirkus Reviews*

"Ward's novel brilliantly evokes both revulsion and a less obvious, but more ominous, sense of dread, as everything we take for granted is called into question. . . . Ward depicts LGBTQ people as we are in real life—complicated, nuanced, and not excited about wading to school through ankle-deep blood." —AfterEllen.com

"Dark, gory, and impossible to put down. A worthy addition to the horror genre!" —Gretchen McNeil,
author of *Ten* and the Don't Get Mad series

"Morbid, gruesome, and viscerally scary—this story made my skin crawl." —Amy Lukavics, author of *Daughters unto Devils*

"This seriously creepy story will draw in horror fans immediately." —*VOYA*

BLEEDING EARTH

KAITLIN WARD

ADAPTIVE BOOKS

AN IMPRINT OF ADAPTIVE STUDIOS
CULVER CITY, CA

Copyright © 2016 Kaitlin Ward
This paperback edition published in 2016.

Visit us on the web at www.adaptivestudios.com

Library of Congress Cataloging-in-Publication Number: 015947213
ISBN 978-1-945293-06-1
Ebook ISBN 978-0-996488-71-6

Printed in the United States of America.
Designed by Christina Quintero

Adaptive Books
3578 Hayden Avenue, Suite 6
Culver City, CA 90232

10 9 8 7 6 5 4 3 2 1

To my parents, who have always been my biggest supporters, and who I would trust to see me safely through the bloodpocalypse.

1.

I drape my arm around a towerlike gravestone, watching my best friend hover at the cemetery's edge. She's lived across from this graveyard her entire life, and still, she's terrified of it. Like skeletons might crawl out from the coffins below the soil and wrap their bony fingers around her ankles.

"Hillary, come *on*!" I shout. "I promise, the cemetery will not hurt you."

She takes a grudging step forward.

I gasp theatrically and stumble like something's just grabbed me. She shrieks and shuffles back toward the edge of the road.

"You're so easy it's almost not even fun," I say, laughing.

She glares at me, sweeping fawn-colored bangs away from her eyes. "I so do not love you right now."

"Just get over here so we can get this done."

I'm torn between exasperation and amusement. Hillary truly is terrified of cemeteries. She's not faking to be cute or whatever. But I'm only so patient, and we're here for a reason. *Her* reason. She's getting tracings of the gravestones of her local ancestors as part of her family history project.

At first she takes baby steps into the cemetery, tugging anxiously on her lip ring. We both have them; we dared each other last year, to the non-amusement of our mothers.

Finally, she makes it past the first row of graves, striding toward me with intense purpose. I consider pretending to be attacked by a dead person again, but decide it's not in my best interest to traumatize her more.

"See?" I smile when she reaches me. "Still alive."

"Oh hush. And hold this."

She hands me a fat crayon, its wrapper peeled off. Then she holds the tracing paper over the face of a gravestone. I rub the side of the crayon back and forth over it until I have a cerulean outline surrounding the name and dates of one of Hillary's ancestors.

We move on to the next, and the next. She's still tense, but I'm kind of enjoying this. It's April; we haven't had much spring so far, and today is so warm, I almost wore my flip-flops for the first time this year. The new grass surrounding the graves is an enthusiastic shade of green, and the brook that runs through the cemetery is swollen with melted snow. I'm just happy to be outdoors, even if it's here.

We've wandered pretty far in now, but the longer we're among the graves without incident, the more Hillary relaxes. Her shoulders lose their arch of tension; her eyes stop darting around like she's expecting to see a ghost. She even starts making jokes about the names of her ancestors.

"Immersion therapy," I tell her. "We should come here every day and cure your fear."

She laughs. "Maybe."

I scrub the crayon over her last piece of tracing paper. She admires our work and rolls it up carefully around the outside of all the others.

"Ms. Hartman better give me an A on this project," she says, patting the smooth granite top of the gravestone.

"I'm sure she will. And you survived the cemetery. No creepy dead girls sprang forth from their eternal resting places to drag you to the underworld."

She smirks. "So far."

We start back toward her house, which perches on a small hill across the street. I wish we could go hiking now, since it's such a beautiful day, but if I even hint at suggesting it, she'll get all guilty and cancel her already-made plans with her boyfriend. She's really weird about putting friends before relationships. Which is nice, except when it loses her the boyfriend.

When we were in ninth grade, she saw something on TV about how you'll regret lost friendships more than lost romantic opportunities, and she's really taken it to heart. I think she's probably right; no one has impacted my life more than my best friend. But her last boyfriend broke up with her after she cancelled three dates in a row for friend "emergencies," and I don't want to be the cause if it happens again. Sometimes I wonder if she doesn't use this whole friends-first-no-matter-what idea to keep them from getting too close. If maybe falling in love is scary. She rolls her eyes and changes the subject any time I suggest such a thing, though.

We've almost reached the front of the cemetery when I step in something mushy. This far from the stream, I wasn't paying attention for mud.

"Hey, Hill, look out, it's . . ." I trail off because what's smeared on the heel of my shoe isn't mud. It's darker. It's red.

"What happened?" Hillary's voice has an edge again.

"I don't know. Something weird's on my shoe."

I crouch and inspect the ground. The grass is slick with a reddish-copper substance.

"Blood," I say aloud. "I just stepped in fucking blood."

"What the hell?" Hillary squats beside me. "Dude. Look, it's all over."

She's right. Blood is oozing up out of the ground in front of this gravestone. Tiny beads like grisly dewdrops, glittering on the bright blades of grass. The longer I look, the plumper the beads become. They push together, forming miniature blood puddles.

"Is this even possible?" I back away slowly, toward the road, toward Hillary's house.

"I don't know. Could the grave be . . . fresh?"

I wrinkle my nose. It's a recently erected stone, but they take the blood out of corpses before they bury them. Don't they? I ask Hillary, and she just shrugs. "Like I know anything about science."

Neither of us are destined to become biologists, that's for sure.

A cloud crosses the sun, cooling both the temperature and my already declining mood.

"We should tell someone," I say. I've scrubbed my foot through the dirt at the side of the road over and over, but it's only smudging the blood. I'm going to have to bleach these shoes. Or throw them out.

"I told you the cemetery was creepy," Hillary grumbles as we wait for cars to pass.

"This is not normal cemetery shit."

We run across the street, up Hillary's driveway, and through her front door. Inside, it smells like peppermint because her mom has an obsession with candles. Hillary's eight-year-old brother is shrieking delightedly from his bedroom upstairs, and her cat eyes me disdainfully before prancing out of sight, as if he cannot be bothered to even waste his eyesight on these foolish human teens.

"Mom!" Hillary calls, slipping out of her shoes.

"In the kitchen!" her mom shouts back.

We skid into the shiny-tiled kitchen in our socks. Hillary's mom is setting out chocolate chip cookies on a cooling rack. They smell heavenly but look, well, I'll say iffy, to be nice. I take one anyway, when she offers them to us. It tastes okay.

"Mom." Hillary leans her elbows on the kitchen's island. "There's blood in the cemetery. Like, a lot. Lea stepped in it."

"Near one of the newer headstones," I add, as though this information is relevant. "It seemed like it was oozing out of the ground."

It sounds so, so stupid now that we're in this peppermint-and-cookie-scented kitchen, away from the gravestone. And Hillary's mom is a nurse, which makes me feel even more stupid. She sees blood all the time.

"Probably a coyote got something," she says.

"I don't know, Mom." Hillary's brow furrows. "It was a lot of blood."

"Do you want me to go look with you?"

Her tone makes me feel even dumber. It's the tone moms use when you're worried about a monster under your bed. The tone they still use sometimes when you're seventeen, but only when they think you're acting like you've lost ten years off your age.

"I guess not." Hillary glances at the oven clock and her eyes widen. "Shit! Shoot, I mean." The amendment is in response to receiving the Look from her mother. "Levi will be here in fifteen minutes."

"I'll head out," I tell her.

"You're sure you don't want a ride home?"

I wave her off. "I know you want to change before he gets here. It's nice out. Walking's good for me."

"Oh yeah. And maybe you'll run into—" Hillary cuts herself off, but I hear the end of her sentence in my head—*Aracely*. We don't talk about my relationships. Not in front of her mom, anyway. I'm out at school, and my parents have known for over a year, but Hillary's parents would so not be okay with the idea that their daughter's best friend dates girls.

"Oh, is there a *boy*?" Hillary's mom asks, catching on—or so she thinks.

"I'm leaving now," I say, but I give a coy smile so she'll think I'm just shy about a crush. This way she won't bring it up again for a long while, and I won't have to lie about anything. Or worse, tell the truth.

"I'll text you," Hillary says, heading for the stairs as I head for the door.

As I walk down the driveway in my defiled shoes, Levi is just pulling up. I tug my phone from my pocket and text, *Better change quickly!*

Levi smiles hesitantly at me as he parks. Hillary's been dating him for a few months now, and he's still kind of uncertain around me. I actually think he views me as competition, which is hilarious, because Hillary couldn't be more straight if she tried.

He isn't a bad-looking guy. He's got the standard blond-haired, blue-eyed thing going on, and he plays sports, so he's in shape. He's always polite, and I heard him make a pretty good joke once. But our distrust is mutual I guess, because there's something about him that bothers me. I just can't settle on *what*.

I don't glance toward the cemetery as I walk down the adjacent road. Great—now I've picked up Hillary's irrational fear. It's just, even thinking about something being killed and leaving behind so much blood unnerves me. And then there was the way the blood seemed to ooze. It wasn't right.

All in all, I'm glad when I reach Main Street's wide sidewalks. It's a pleasant twenty-five-minute walk from Hillary's house to mine, and a bonus of spring is that there are few tourists. Skiing is done, leaf-peeping is long done, and summer tourist traps haven't yet opened. Which means Main Street is blissfully free of fanny packs and of iPads being used as cameras. And Hillary was right; I *am* hoping to maybe possibly run into Aracely, whose apartment is at the other end of Main Street.

Aracely and I have only been on a few dates, but I'm already falling pretty hard. I barely knew her before; she's a junior, and we don't have any overlap in our circles of friends, but we had a class together last semester. I noticed her—how could I not?—but she's not out, so other than a couple wistful daydreams, I didn't give any thought to dating her. Until the day she came up to me and asked me out.

I pass by a church that recently upgraded its inspirational quotes sign to an LED display with bright pink bulbs. Usually, I don't pay it much mind, but today they have up the absolute creepiest quote I have ever seen.

Beloveds, don't be afraid, it reads, and there's something so chilling about reading those words in that cheerfully bright lettering.

I take a picture of it with my phone because this needs to be texted to every single friend I have.

I'm captioning my message when someone across the street screams. It's the kind of scream that digs into my bones and nestles in the marrow, echoing as pulses of fear in my nerves.

And then there's shouting. Not where I heard the scream, but farther down Main Street, where the shops are. I can't tell what's happening, what's getting to everyone. They're all backing toward the storefronts. Mothers are picking up their children. A parked police car turns on its lights.

I creep backward onto the church steps, looking around wildly for a hint about what's wrong. No one's clustering together. People aren't fleeing just one spot, either; they're panicking all over. Edging into stores or sitting atop the hoods of cars.

It's the sidewalk people are pointing at. The sidewalk they're abandoning in droves.

But the sidewalk's fine. It's—

It's not fine.

Holy shit.

I crouch carefully on the bottom step, peering down. There's something red seeping up through the cracks between slabs of the sidewalk. Spilling over and dripping onto the street. It's impossible and it's insane, and part of me thinks I'm having a hallucination.

Beloveds, don't be afraid, the sign still proclaims brightly beside me.

But I am. I am suddenly so afraid that the fear becomes a white-hot brand, pressed into my heart. And I should be, because something impossible is happening.

The earth is bleeding.

2.

Mom and I have boxed mac and cheese for dinner because neither of us wants to leave the living room long enough to cook a real meal.

The blood I saw today was only the beginning. It's happening everywhere. Everywhere in the entire world.

Nothing's on TV but this. Right now, they're showing footage of somewhere in Antarctica. Cameras meant to watch the behavior of seals caught it all as the clear-white ice slowly blushed pink, and then oozed beads of red.

I get up and look out the picture window. Our lawn is scarlet. It's only a thin, squelchy layer, but it's there. In the hazy light of dusk, I can almost pretend it's just spring-melted snow. But I saw it earlier, in its horror-movie reality. Blood settles in a more viscous way than water. It doesn't just drown the grass—it suffocates it.

I've thrown up three times since I've gotten home, and looking out the window makes my stomach waver again. I turn away.

A scientist is talking now on the news. It can't be blood, he says. It's impossible for the earth to bleed, he says. And then he launches into a description of every blood-looking substance it could be. But, he says, even if it is blood—and of course it isn't, but if it *was*—we shouldn't be worried, and here are all sorts of reasons why.

I don't feel soothed.

Especially when, like it's an afterthought, he warns that we should still be careful not to touch it. Don't touch it, but don't worry, because really, everything is going to be fine.

If everything is going to be fine, why is this on every channel? Why has the president already made a grim-faced speech about carrying on and using caution until "the situation" is resolved? Why are religious fanatics setting up camps and preparing for the end of days? Why has school been cancelled for the whole of next week?

I sit back down beside Mom. She squeezes my hand.

"I wish you'd been home when it started," she says.

"Me, too."

I should have let Hillary drive me this afternoon when she offered. But how could I ever have known? The shoes I wore today are in the trash. I scrubbed them until my fingers were raw, but all I accomplished was to push the blood deeper into the fibers. They're unfixable now.

"Maybe we could do something besides watch the news," I suggest. "We could cook Dad a really great dinner."

Mom clutches the remote, running her fingers over its rubbery buttons. "I suppose we could."

"It'll be fun," I urge. "And he'll be wicked happy."

I swear to God, it's like I'm their marriage counselor. They never do anything nice for each other unless I suggest it, and then they wonder why they don't get along anymore.

"Okay. But we'll leave the TV on so we can check it in between."

Mom loves to cook. Once I shepherd her into the kitchen, she seems to forget all about the news. It's the nicest room in our house by far; my parents spent tons of money on a double oven, stainless steel gas stovetop, and a billion cooking accessories most people wouldn't even recognize.

Mom used to cook elaborate meals for the three of us. She

still cooks elaborate meals most of the time—for her and me. Dad gets leftovers, which he has to reheat himself. He never complains. But it must bother him. It bothers me.

Their unhappiness didn't come in a moment. It didn't come in fits of screaming and threats of violence. It doesn't even look like unhappiness, probably, from outside our family. Sometimes I wish they would scream. Instead, they live in this cocoon of indifferent silence.

So it makes me happy, watching Mom prepare a meal for Dad. It's probably stupid to hold out hope that they can one day rediscover their feelings for each other, but I do hope it.

Otherwise it's just sad. They're determined not to get a divorce—some remnant of Mom's religious upbringing—and I hate watching them live these half-lives because of their stubbornness.

I'm helping Mom with a side salad when headlights sweep across the window. Dad's home. He has worked at the dam since before I was born. His hours have always been long, but today, with this mess, he was stuck even later than usual. There's a lot that goes into getting electricity from a dam to our houses, and the last thing we need right now is for people to lose power. That's what he told me earlier, anyway, when he called to say he'd be late.

Once inside, Dad kicks off his bloodstained work boots with a disgusted expression.

"We made dinner," I say.

Mom pokes her head out of the kitchen. "It's just about ready."

"Wow," says Dad. "Thank you."

"It was Lea's idea."

God, shut up, Mom.

"But Mom's the one who decided what to make."

Veal parmesan, his favorite, which he almost never gets to eat because I steadfastly refuse to eat baby animals.

Dad smiles in Mom's general direction. Which I'm calling a win.

"Before I eat, I'm going to fill some buckets with water. And the bathtub," he says.

"Why?" I ask.

"In case the—in case something gets into our water supply."

I roll my eyes. Like if he says "something," I won't know he means blood. But he misinterprets my eye roll.

"This is serious, Lea. I'm not being doomsday. There's a very real problem out there. You should've seen the traffic. People are panicking, and with good reason."

"I know; that wasn't what—never mind."

He and Mom share a Lea-is-being-difficult look over my head. Win number two of the evening, I guess. Even if it's at my expense.

"I'll do it. You eat," I say. "How many buckets?"

Dad smiles. "Thanks, Lea. As many as you can find."

I fill bucket after bucket. Bowl after bowl. Mom brings me anything we have that could possibly hold water. I line them up in the hall. I really do not like the idea that blood could start running from our water pipes. While filling the bathtub, I keep a close eye out for any hints of color. Nothing. Thank God.

Still, I picture it, blood seeping down into the ground, settling into wells and lakes with our water, flowing out of faucets. Dad didn't say it was happening yet—and wouldn't he know, working right there on the river?—but that doesn't mean it won't. I hadn't considered how deeply this could invade our lives, and as more pieces snap into the puzzle, I'm starting to wonder how the president could've possibly told us to carry on. Even just on a basic level, how are we going to bathe, if we have to store water in our bathtub? Wash our clothes, if it gets worse? If this lasts longer than a matter of days, we're in real trouble.

I squint at the bathtub water again because I thought I saw a blush of pink, but nothing's there. Just clear, normal water, and my imagination getting out of control.

When I'm finally done, I plop onto the couch next to Mom and Dad, who are watching the news again.

"Your phone did something while you were in the bathroom," says Mom.

"Oh, thanks." I pick it up. Texts from Hillary and Aracely. *Aracely!*

My stomach clenches in a swirl of excitement and anxiety as I open Aracely's.

Hope ur ok! it says.

With an exclamation mark, even.

I'm fine, you?

It's embarrassing how long it takes me to type that. And how long it takes to convince myself to hit SEND. I should've texted her earlier. I wanted to, but I'm forever nervous of scaring her off.

Hill's text is longer. Profuse apologies for not driving me home. I tell her it's fine, and for the rest of the evening, we text about how her date with Levi went, analyze what it means that Aracely texted just to check on me, and speculate how long school will actually be closed. She and Levi left her house only minutes after I did, so they experienced the same shock as me when blood started seeping out of the ground. She was stuck at Levi's for hours because traffic got backed up by all the people trying to get home. She didn't sound like she was too bummed about it, though. I wouldn't have been, if I were "stuck" at Aracely's.

"Who're you texting?" Mom asks with this knowing little smirk on her face.

"Hillary," I say, and it comes out sounding much more defiant than I mean for it to.

"*Just* Hillary?" Mom's voice is laced with teasing.

Dad peeks around her and he has that same smirk, like it's just so adorable that I'm dating someone, which is maybe because even though I've been out to them for a while, Aracely is the first girlfriend I've told them about. I'm starting to regret it. Parents teasing you about your girlfriend is pretty high up on the list of life's worst embarrassments.

"Oh my God, Mom. Do I ask you who *you're* texting all the time?"

Both of them sit back against the couch and flick their gazes back to the TV in synchronization, and if they can pretend this conversation never happened, so can I.

The TV continues to blare the same non-news it's been reporting all evening. Basically, it's just more scientists dissecting the possibilities—what's happening, how long it'll last. And it's stupid because clearly, they don't know.

More footage of people panicking, of insane traffic jams, of people sobbing and reading Bible passages. There are some scary-cool images, too: more icy places blushed red, blood rolling down hillsides, white-sanded deserts turned crimson. But I'm having trouble reconciling these images with reality. This is a thing that is happening. In real life. In my town. On my planet. It's crazy. Impossible. It feels like an elaborate hoax. My brain refuses to accept the truth of this no matter the evidence, and mulling it over starts to give me a headache.

"I'm going to bed," I announce. My parents are engrossed—they'll be up for a while.

I'm going to sleep and hope that in the morning this will all be nothing but a memory.

3.

Between Mother Nature and human nature, disasters are inevitable. Hurricanes and tornadoes and tsunamis and earthquakes all seem to be in an endless battle to outdo themselves. Sometimes creepy things happen, like birds falling dead, inexplicably, from the sky, or spiders raining down from above. People are stuck in a cycle of ever-increasing brutality with bombings and wars and shootings, each incident making less sense than the last.

But this.

This makes less sense than any of it.

We don't even know what it *is* yet. If it's blood, whose blood is it? And if it's not, what could it be? Of course, the question that supersedes them all is *why*, and that's the one it seems least likely we'll get an answer to.

We can't rescue people from it, because it's *everywhere*. There are no safe zones for evacuation, not anywhere on the entire planet. We're just as screwed here in New Hampshire as they are in Zimbabwe or Brazil or even the arctic, for Christ's sake. So we're waiting; school's closed for the foreseeable future, as are most workplaces considered unessential—like Mom's. There was so much panic yesterday, and there still is. But it's died down, because it accomplished nothing. There's nowhere to go, nothing to do. We just have to give it time. Of course, waiting is its own special kind of hell.

It's three hours into Monday, and I'm so bored, I already wish for school to reopen. Well played, universe. Well played.

"Lea!" Mom calls to me.

I drag myself away from my laptop and peer out of my room. "What?"

"We're going to the grocery store."

"Why do I have to come?"

"Because."

Oh, *because*. That's a compelling reason. Maybe she realizes it isn't enough, because she pops into the hallway and adds, "I might need your help. We'll want to be well-stocked until this . . . ends."

I don't like the way she says *ends*. The way her voice hooks on to the word and gives it meanings she hopes I don't hear. I don't want to do this. The idea of needing to be well-stocked, I just . . . I still feel like I'm in a play or something. This isn't *life*.

"Fine. I'll come."

Mom grabs her keys, pulls on her boots and a coat. I follow suit. Reluctantly.

Traffic is unbelievably bad. It's disgusting outside. There's no other way to spin this. The blood is ankle-deep now. Yesterday it was an inch at most. I don't like it. Don't like the warmth, the thickness, the way it gets everywhere and refuses to drain like floodwaters would.

I wonder about Aracely, if she's trapped in her apartment, or if she and her dad might be grocery shopping, too. And I wonder about my friends, if their houses are holding up. Ours hasn't been penetrated by blood yet, but Hillary's has that spot where the basement floods every spring, and Cadence lives in a trailer . . .

Mom starts driving, and it distracts me from my thoughts. The tires splash through the streets like we're in a shallow river. We hit a pothole and send up a spray of red. A cacophony of blaring horns echoes from down on Main Street, and it takes twenty minutes to drive the quarter-mile from our house to the end of our road—so Mom opts for the nearby food co-op over the larger grocery store that's on the other side of town. When we pull into the parking lot, it's already full. Overfull. People have parked in all sorts of creative ways.

Lucky for us, someone's pulling out just as we arrive, and we're rewarded with a spot near the store entrance.

Mom is pale and tight-lipped as she gets a cart, steering it through the grimy waves of blood.

"What do we do if it doesn't go away?" I ask, swirling my toe in it. The motion stirs up sediment, and it looks even grosser.

Mom says nothing.

Her silence is worse than anything she could have said. When she doesn't think I'll like her answer, she says nothing at all. Like when I was nine and I split my chin open on the heating grate. I asked her if I'd need stitches. She herded me into the car, pressing a cloth beneath my chin, and didn't say a word the whole way to the hospital.

I ended up with eight stitches.

The co-op is crowded. It reminds me of the night before an anticipated storm, when everyone's making sure they'll have plenty of food if they can't leave their homes for six days or something. I guess this *is* kind of like a storm. The store is electric with urgency. I feel unsettled; my muscles coil with the sense that I have to get somewhere *right this second*, except I don't know where or why.

The floor is slippery, slicked with blood that spills

inside every time the doors open. Farther in, it's better, but smeared with tracks from people's feet.

Mom mumbles to herself as she piles canned goods into our cart from shelves that are looking a little bare. A woman practically body slams me out of the way so she can scoop up an armful of canned lima beans—like I would ever voluntarily eat lima beans. I give her the dirtiest look I can muster, and she glares back at me with equal vehemence. I consider snatching one of her cans of beans, but she seems like she might claw out my eyes if I did.

In the next aisle, I peer to the back of a nearly empty shelf, curious what was here, and reach for the one box still crammed into the back. I've almost tugged it out when a man steals it from my grasp.

"Hey!" I protest, but he is already barreling his overloaded cart toward the checkout counter.

I start to ask Mom what everyone's problem is today, but she interrupts loudly, "Which brand of granola do you think looks best?"

Which one looks the best? How about none of them. I narrow my eyes and pluck a random bag off the shelf.

"Grab a few, please," she says.

Many of the aisles are almost completely wiped of products. I've seen grocery stores look like this in pictures—after hurricanes and that sort of thing. But not here, never here. We're resourceful. We don't fly into panic mode and empty out our stores before big meteorological crises because we can take care of ourselves. We can drive in the snow and the ice and the rain. We own attire for every season. Hell, if all else fails, I don't know anyone who doesn't know someone who hunts.

I don't understand what's happening here in this grocery store.

"This is taking too long," Mom says. Her voice is taut. "You get toilet paper, and I'll meet you by the milk."

She takes off before I can tell her that I don't want to be separated. I've never seen this store so full, never seen people so aggressive. It's a food co-op, for Christ's sake. Usually, it's a breeze, if you avoid elderly ladies taking up whole aisles with their carts, or hippies who just cannot debate about animal rights anywhere but directly in front of the deli counter.

I grab a couple individual rolls of toilet paper since they're all that's left, and start to turn back up the aisle, but then I stop, because something catches my eye. Tampons. If the toilet paper's absence is any indication, those might soon be hard to come by, and I sure as hell don't want to run out. Three boxes remain, and I take them all.

"You have to *share*," a girl says from behind me.

I whirl to face her. She's college-aged, maybe, sort of pretty, definitely pissed off.

"This is a grocery store," I say coolly. "Not kindergarten."

She reaches for one of my boxes, but I turn sideways. She reaches again, and I elbow her in the gut.

"Bitch!" she shouts after me as I disappear into the crowd. A shiver runs through me when I think about what I've done. Just the smallest act of violence, but now I have no moral high ground over the others in here, who I was so disdainful toward just moments ago.

I get to the milk, but Mom isn't there. Nor is any milk, except a half-gallon that's fallen and is belching its contents onto the floor while a man and a woman shout at each other over the top of it.

"Lea!" I hear Mom shouting; I think she's at the opposite side of the aisle.

I start toward her, but I'm in the midst of a crush of people, all hurrying, fast-fingered, edgy. I can't break loose because they're packed so tightly, and I don't want any of them to wrest my supplies away.

I panic. Which is stupid. It isn't like I've never been alone in a store before.

"Coming, Mom!" I call back, and hurry toward the sound of her voice, flowing with the crowd as best I can.

Someone slams their cart into my hip, pinning me against one of the freezer doors. It's an older lady, wearing a pantsuit. She doesn't even apologize. I'm starting to get really pissed off, and I still don't know where my mom is, so I kick roughly at the cart. It hurts, but I manage to upend it, and pantsuit lady drops to the floor, chasing her spilled items.

"Sorry," I say, my voice harsh and unrecognizable.

And that's when I get it: the thing that's different. The reason we're emptying out a grocery store and wrestling over lima beans and slamming into teenage girls with shopping carts.

We're not just preparing for a disaster.

We're preparing for an apocalypse.

4.

I revisit the food co-op in my dreams. Nightmares, I should say. I've always been the sort of person who has colorful, vivid dreams, but this is much darker than anything my mind's come up with before.

I'm separated from my mom, and I can't find her. The co-op's aisles grow longer and longer. I'm supposed to be grabbing something, but all the shelves are empty and I'm surrounded by faceless people with empty shopping carts. I start to run, screaming for Mom as I do, but the faster I run, the longer the aisle gets, so I slow down, and then.

The aisle ends. I turn up the next, and it's even more crowded, because these shelves aren't empty and maybe I'll finally find Mom. I glance up at the shelf to my right because I'm also supposed to be getting something and she'll probably be mad if I don't find it, but what's on the shelf isn't what I'm supposed to find. Not at all.

What's on the shelf is parts. Human parts. Eyeballs, which keep swerving to watch passersby. A twitching, dismembered hand. A torso with a hole in it where the heart should be. A skull. A foot. A messy pile of glistening intestines. And, on the highest shelf, a heart. Still pumping. Spitting out blood with each thump, sending it splashing down onto the lower shelves in a waterfall that forms a pool of blood around my feet.

I wake when my stomach lurches, and roll immediately to my side, reaching for the trash can beside my bed. I gag over it, hard, twice, but manage to keep the contents of my stomach where they belong.

And then I lay shivering and sweating in my bed, tears stinging my eyes, long into the night.

I wake up early, to the sound of my alarm, and leap out of bed. I want to catch Dad before he leaves for work. And I do; he's sitting on the couch with a bowl of cereal, watching the news.

"Are you home today?" I ask, sitting beside him.

He shakes his head. "It'll probably be long hours again. There's a lot of work going into keeping the transformers at the power station from being compromised, and keeping the river from flooding too high on either end."

I picture the dam, open, with water rushing down its back wall. I've always thought it looked so dangerous, so *powerful*, when it did that. The big structure of concrete actually controls a river. That's badass. But I don't like picturing it doing the same thing with water turned dark from blood—which could happen. I overheard Mom and Dad talking about it; Dad said they're starting to notice a slight discoloration, a little extra volume to the water. I don't like that idea, either: the notion that dams might have trouble regulating the water soon because of this extra liquid. What about all the fish and the other creatures that live under there? Are they okay? Or are their gills poisoned by the blood, like filthy pollution?

"Is it safe for you to go out there?" I ask.

It takes him a long moment to answer me. He fills his mouth with an overflowing spoonful of cereal, losing a droplet of milk onto his beard. "I don't know," he says finally, and I appreciate his honesty. "But if we can't keep the power on, it'll get much worse, much more quickly."

He gestures to the TV, which shows images of some city

where people are full-on rioting. All the buildings are dark; wherever it is, they've lost power already.

"They say," Dad continues, "that with a major disaster, the cities suffer first, and often hardest. We've got less people out here, and more resources, funny as that sounds. It'll take a while for this to hit us as badly. By then, hopefully it'll all be over with." He pats my arm. "Don't worry about all this, okay, Lea?"

"Okay," I say softly.

He gets up and sets his cereal bowl in the sink. I stay on the couch and watch the news while he packs himself a lunch. I should offer to help, maybe, since I have nothing to do all day and he has to go out there. But I don't feel like helping, because I really don't want him to go, and there's a foolish, childish part of me that thinks maybe if I look forlorn enough, he'll stay.

He doesn't.

After he's finished packing his lunch, he kisses my cheek, laces up his boots, and he's gone.

I go to the picture window and watch him back his truck out of the driveway. I can't tell if the blood is deeper now than it was yesterday; it's deep enough to completely engulf our lawn's well-trimmed grass, that's all I know.

"Be careful," I whisper, curling my fingers into the windowsill.

I hate this feeling of worry that's taken up residence inside me. Hate the way last night's dream still lingers, a vile whisper in the back of my mind. The way I'm curious about the blood, in spite of my revulsion. Which, in turn, makes me feel even more repulsed.

I tear my gaze from the mess outdoors with a full-body shudder.

It hits me then, how Dad described the situation. Without power, it'd get worse *much more quickly*, he said. So he thinks it's going to get worse, then, regardless. He's just trying to slow it down.

The way he's accepted it, so stoically, like there was always a possibility something like this might happen one day . . . that might be the most terrifying thing of all.

5.

School reopens after a week. Here, anyway. For now, the blood doesn't appear to be going anywhere, so as unpleasant as it is, schools and workplaces around here have decided we should just carry on as though everything's normal. We can do that, because we still have power, we still have resources.

Some areas remain shut down. Cities, mostly, and ultra-flooded places near the coast. Rural areas are doing okay, generally, but people have drowned in subway stations and with most of their mass transit unavailable for the time being, some of the larger cities are struggling to remain functional. It's terrifying. I can't even imagine what it must feel like to live someplace like New York right now. All those people, unable to go anywhere, to do anything. Places like that were the first to lose power, and they haven't gotten it back. I try to picture living through this without being able to leave my house, without even being able to learn what's happening on the news because there's no electricity, and the thought is so scary I have to push it back to the darkest recesses of my mind. The part that protects me during the day from all the things I don't want to think about, but betrays me at night with ever-escalating nightmares.

Of course, since we *don't* have power outages and flooded transportation systems, I am forced to walk to school like it's any other Monday. Even though blood follows me down the hill, undulating in rivulets like water during a heavy rainstorm. And it's definitely blood. I don't care what the idiot scientists on the news keep saying. I see it, I smell it. I've never seen so much at once, but I know what it is.

I don't look down as I cross the bridge over the river, and I have to brace myself against a just-higher-than-ankle-deep flow while I wait at the stoplight to cross Main Street. Heading uphill toward school is going to be hellish, I have a feeling.

"God, this is disgusting," says a voice beside me.

It's Aracely. I smile warmly at her, both anxious and pleased to see her. She returns the expression, flashing me her square, white teeth. My nerves multiply, and I can't feel my fingertips. It's been nine days since I've seen her, and I'm so excited that my walk gets all bouncy, like my legs want to hop toward her, and I'm totally aware of how not attractive it is, but my body has stopped listening to my brain.

Aracely lives in an apartment that overlooks the river, in the building on this corner. I have to walk this way to get to school no matter what, but I'd be lying if I said I didn't start leaving a few minutes earlier in the mornings once we started dating. We're too new—and too secret—to walk to school together every day on purpose, but if it just happens to work out that way . . . well, I'm not complaining.

"Yeah, disgusting is one way to put it," I say, trying not to look down at the liquid warming my feet through my boots.

"Can you believe they reopened school?"

"I can't believe they reopened *anything*."

"It's a pride thing, I think," she says, and she's right. Other parts of the country—of the world—are pulling themselves together and carrying on despite it all, so we can, too. Anything less would be shameful.

The WALK light flashes, and we hurry across the street.

The blood is sort of . . . gelatinous, almost. Walking through it isn't like wading through a puddle of water. It resists. And it smells terrible. Metallic, but also rancid. This has to be unhealthy for our lungs. Plus, now it's starting to feel weirdly spongy beneath my feet. That can't be right.

I won't look down at it, don't *want* to look.

I look at Aracely instead. Out of the corner of my eye so she won't think I'm being weird. She's so, so pretty. She's shorter than me, though not by much. Her eyes are dark and so is her hair, which falls in loose curls well below her shoulders.

My hair is black, too—well, blackish. But our similarities end there. My cheeks are freckled and my eyes are a bright shade of green. I've always felt all right about how I look. But I'm not nearly so pretty as Aracely, who is trim and fit but somehow still manages to have the sort of curves straight-hipped girls like me could only dream of.

I also think she looks a whole lot less ridiculous in her rubber boots than I do in mine. Maybe it's because mine are swamp colored, and hers are much cuter—black with red stripes.

Red. Like the blood I will not look at that is leaking through imaginary holes that do not exist in my boots. I don't want to see my feet sloshing through it. I really, really don't.

I look.

A bubble forms and pops near my feet as I reach the sidewalk on the other side of the street. Wait. That's new. I think.

"Do you see that?" I point. "Is that normal?"

Aracely throws me an exasperated look. "I don't know. Is it normal for the streets to be filled with fucking blood?"

But then she stops, gripping a telephone pole as she leans closer to the bubbling. She lifts a foot, catching something across the toe of her boot. "Oh Jesus." She recoils in horror. "Is that . . . ?"

My stomach churns. "Hair."

It's rising in patches now, belched to the surface by the frothing blood.

"Come on." Aracely grabs my arm, turning the opposite direction of school, jabbing at the WALK button on the stoplight. Her expression is grim, her mouth pressed into a worried line.

"Come where?"

"Back inside. This is ridiculous. We're not going to school."

"But we—I—" I give up. Hair clings to my boots, and blood covers the planet. School shouldn't have reopened in the first place.

So I follow Aracely back across the street. There's an awkward moment where I'm not sure if she means for me to go with her to her apartment or return to my house, alone, but when I hesitate, she grabs my hand and pulls me through the door to her building. She's so decisive. I envy and appreciate it.

Our rain boots leave red stains as we stomp up the stairs and down the hallway. I'm sure trails of hair follow us, too, but I can't bear to look behind me. Thinking about it nearly makes me ill. Aracely pauses outside the door of her apartment. "Let's, uh, leave our boots out here."

We both remove our footwear in the same way: gripping them only by their tops, hopping away from them like they're poison. Aracely unlocks the door, and I let out a breath, relieved to be in here with no blood in sight.

I love her apartment. She hates it because the neighbors are loud and the floors, creaky. But it's hardwood and has an open layout and big windows that overlook the river. *Really* overlook it, because this building is perched on the edge of the water. It's over a hundred years old and marks the end of Main Street, curving around to meet the bridge that crosses the river. Looking down out the window at the rushing water below gives me a breathless, excited feeling, like standing with my toes at the edge of a cliff.

Right away, Aracely excuses herself to the bathroom. I hear her in there, puking. I think this is one of those moments where I'm supposed to prove my worth as a girlfriend and hold back her hair, but no way in hell I'm going in there. Else there'll be two of us vomiting. I'm barely keeping down my breakfast as it is.

When the toilet flushes, I grab a bottle of water from the fridge and knock gently on the bathroom door. She pushes it open from her seat on the floor in front of the toilet.

"Sorry," she says scratchily.

"I don't blame you."

I hand her the water, which she sips slowly. This should be a great opportunity for us. We're alone—*very* alone—with several hours ahead of us. We barely get to see each other, usually. She works after school most days, doing paperwork and such at the garage where her dad's a mechanic, and she can't spend every moment of her free time with me, or else her friends would get suspicious. But I'm too shaken right now to appreciate our situation the way I'd like.

"Should we watch the news?" Aracely asks hesitantly.

"Yeah, good idea."

We sit on the couch, close but not touching, and turn on the TV. They're showing footage of the hair. I hope it doesn't make Aracely sick again.

She seems okay. Her eyes don't leave the screen while she pops a mint into her mouth. I'm trying to decide what it means that she didn't offer me one when my phone beeps. It's a text from Hillary: *Where. Are. You????*

At Aracely's, I type back. *The hair on the street was gross so we're skipping.*

I know she's going to be annoyed about this. I haven't seen her in over a week. But she'll have to understand.

A list of countries scrolls down the screen. Countries where hair has been spotted. It's a long list.

"Can you even believe that this is news right now?" Aracely says, shaking her head. "It's unreal."

"Yeah. It's like the earth's rejecting us or something."

My phone beeps with another text from Hillary. *I'm coming over tonight*, it says.

Sure, I reply.

Aracely shuts off the TV. "I know if we're skipping school we should be watching the news," she says. "But I can't. It's too . . ."

"I know."

I squeeze her hand without thinking, and then I start thinking about it and get really nervous. My emotions are so jumbled. Something unfathomably awful is happening out there, but sitting here on Aracely's couch, I feel happy. I can't wrap my mind around the mess outside. I've seen news story after news story, and I've walked through blood and hair with my rain boots on, and still it seems like a strange, twisted nightmare. Like everything I've experienced so far has been some kind of hallucinogenic out-of-body experience.

Aracely rests her head on my shoulder and I'm frustrated because this should all be so simple, but we're not skipping school just to be alone together; we're skipping because walking there was unbearable.

"Do you think we'll die?" she asks, lifting her head from my shoulder.

"What? No! Don't be ridiculous."

To be honest, I hadn't considered the possibility. Should I have? Could it eventually flood higher and higher until all life on earth ceases to exist? No. There's no way. A panicked feeling sets up camp in my chest, manifesting as a painful pressure there, sending tendrils of shaky numbness into my fingertips.

"What if it's like this forever?" Aracely continues. "What if schools teach future generations about that time when there wasn't blood in the streets? What if—"

"Aracely. I mean this in the nicest way possible, but shut up." As soon as I say it, I regret it. "I'm sorry. Look, I don't know, okay? It's scary. I'm scared."

I don't want to talk about it. I don't want this tightening vise of terror clamped on my heart. The idea that things may never be normal again . . . no. It has to go back to normal, because no other alternative is acceptable. Tears press behind my eyes, and my lips tremble with the effort of holding them in. Aracely, inexplicably, grins.

"What are you smiling for?" I ask.

"I thought you weren't afraid. You've been so . . . calm. It was kind of freaking me out."

"I keep things in, I guess." Just saying this gives me that panicked feeling again. "When there's nothing to be done, I mean. The earth bleeding, skipping school . . ." *My parents.* But that, I won't say out loud.

She tilts her head to the side as though pondering this. "Are you telling me that skipping school is worrying you?"

Of all the things. "Um, a little. I've never skipped before. Have you?"

She laughs. "Of course."

"But doesn't the school call your dad? Aren't you worried you'll be in trouble?"

"You just have to be smart about it. I always have a solid excuse for why I skipped, even if it's made up, because then Dad's not pissed. Besides, I bet half our school is home today. They probably won't even bother to call."

"Oh." Suddenly, I feel completely lame. I'm not the only person who never skips school, I remind myself. But it doesn't make me feel any cooler.

"So basically," she says, and I'm not sure when it happened, but she's a lot nearer to me than she was a second ago. "The blood is something to worry about. School? Not so much."

She kisses me. It takes me by surprise, even though it shouldn't, and we're awkward and our mouths are sort of bumping more than kissing. I wonder if this counts as our third date, and if so, if it's a good one or a bad one. Then we find that moment where everything aligns, and the kissing feels like kissing and I decide it's a great one.

Her mouth is warm and soft and her fingers sliding through my hair make my heart beat faster. Pumping blood through my veins. I don't usually think about my blood while kissing. I don't *want* to think about my blood while kissing.

So I kiss her harder, press my hands against the soft skin of her lower back, slide my fingertips up her spine. Her mouth moves to my neck and her fingers graze my ribs and I'm still thinking about blood a little bit, but I kind of don't care anymore.

My phone rings, a harsh sound that completely shatters the moment. It's my mom's ringtone.

"Hi, Mom." I answer it quickly, bracing myself for her wrath. Aracely is half on my lap, her arms still around me, and this does not make it easy to concentrate.

"The school called." Mom doesn't bother with a greeting. "Why aren't you there?"

"Because it's gross. There's blood and hair, and it made me feel sick."

Aracely gives me a thumbs-up. We'll see.

"This isn't like you, Lea. Are you with Hillary? Cadence? Felix? Wait, you must be with that girl you're dating . . . What's her name again?"

"No, no one's with me." I hope I didn't say it too quickly. "I promise this isn't going to become, like, a habit. I just didn't want to be there today. I'm sorry. I know I shouldn't have."

She pauses for a long time, and I nervously twist the hem of Aracely's shirt around my finger. Mom doesn't like to leave early from the collectibles distributor where she works because they have a crazy strict policy about unplanned absences, but if she thinks I'm up to something, she'll come home for sure. Finally, she says, "Okay. As long as you promise it won't happen again. And since you're home, you're in charge of dinner tonight."

"Sure. Of course."

"I'll see you after work, sweetheart."

"Okay. Love you, Mom. Bye."

I hang up with a rough sigh. "I expected that to go a *lot* worse. So long as I'm home and starting dinner by the time she gets out of work at four, we're good."

Aracely grins.

"So obviously the school *is* calling parents today. If they call your dad, is there any chance . . . Would he come home?"

She slides off my lap, which is not what I wanted at all. "I don't think so. He never has before. He needs to save his time off, you know? He doesn't get a whole lot."

I don't want to have to ask her if it's okay if we keep kissing. I want her to get the hint and tell me.

Her dad doesn't know. Not about us, or about her. She says he'd be okay with it, but he would make her tell her grandparents, and she doesn't want to.

They're very elderly, non-English speaking French Canadian, super Catholic, and old-fashioned in all the wrong ways. The racist, homophobic ways. They weren't on speaking terms with Aracely's father from the time he married her Spanish mother until a workplace accident left him a widower a few years ago. Apparently, the relationship remains strained, even now.

I get that Aracely doesn't want to make things harder on her dad, but it makes me sad that she can't be her true self around her own family. Or anyone, really. Her friends don't know, either. I'm not the first girl she's kissed, but I am her first girlfriend, and it wouldn't have happened if she hadn't found me alone one day and asked me out.

She invited me to watch a weird-sounding independent film in a neighboring town, and I was caught so off-guard that I said yes even though weird-sounding films are not my thing. I almost cancelled, even, but Hillary convinced me not to. She can sense things sometimes that I don't even know about my own self—which is what best friends are for, I guess. I'd noticed Aracely in the class we had together. Had even talked to her a little. She seemed smart and fun, and I was jealous of the couple friends of hers who were in the class also. But I never knew, never suspected, that she might've noticed me, too. No matter how many times I'm proved wrong, I still work off this naïve, arrogant assumption that I know everyone who's gay at our school, closeted or not. Aracely's not my first girlfriend; I've had three before her. Two that just fizzled out, one that ended kind of badly. Until the day Aracely surprised me with her movie date idea, I figured I'd be on my own till college, and I was fine with that. I still don't entirely know how she summoned the courage to ask me out, but I'm glad she did.

The moment is seared onto my brain: Aracely approaching me at my locker during a rare moment when I was alone. Her eyes were everywhere but on me, her hands wringing anxiously. "Listen, so, I know you're gay," she'd blurted out. "I mean—that sounded weird. I am, too. No one knows, but I— so there's this film at that theater in Bethlehem tomorrow at seven and maybe you'd . . . go with me?"

My brain buzzed, and I'm pretty sure my jaw actually fell open. She was *asking me out*, was this for real?

"You don't have to," she rushed on. "And if you don't, we can pretend this conversation never happened. I just, we had that class last semester and I thought you were—"

"I'll go. I'd love to." I should have let her finish, but the words burst free. Her face lit up with the most crazy beautiful smile, and even though I barely knew her, I wanted to grab her and kiss her right in the hallway.

"Great," she said breathlessly. "Here's my number. Text me later and we can figure out where to meet and stuff?"

"Okay," I said. She pressed a Post-it note into my palm, lit my nerves on fire, and walked away.

My doubts came later, but Hillary said, "You are going on that date if I have to take you my fucking self," so I decided to see it through. It was only a couple hours, after all, and if it was horrible, I had no obligation to keep things going beyond that.

We were only about fifteen minutes into the movie when Aracely confessed that she actually had zero interest in the film, except it sounded like something no one else from our school would come see. Then I confessed my own disinterest, and we spent the rest of the evening ignoring irritated glances from those around us while we whispered together about the things we actually *did* enjoy.

"Maybe I'll call my dad," Aracely says, bringing me back to the present. "Then I'll know. And either way, you can stay. Just, we might have to pretend . . . you know."

"It's okay," I tell her, and I mean it.

"It isn't. It's not fair to you at all, and I know that."

This time, it's me who closes the space between us. "I knew from the start that this would have to be a secret. If I didn't like it, I didn't have to date you."

She smiles and I kiss her, and all our problems melt away beneath brushes of mouths and fingertips and skin on skin.

She never does end up calling her father.

6.

Hillary arrives at my house approximately two minutes after Mom finishes lecturing me about skipping school. Thank God. The tension in here is thicker than the blood outside.

Hillary throws the front door open wide, standing uncertainly on our tiny porch. The blood has crept high enough now that it laps at our bottom stair. Another couple inches and the stair will be covered.

"Where do you want my boots?" she asks.

"Right on the mat is fine," I answer.

"Hi, Hillary," Mom says stiffly. "How was school?"

"Weird," Hillary says, prying off her boots with a wrinkled nose. "But uneventful."

"Well, it's good that you went. That was the right thing to do," says Mom, with all the subtlety of those people who come talk to us at school about drugs and pregnancy and smoking and whatever. And in case I didn't get it, she throws me a sharp glance before leaving us for the news.

Passive aggressiveness does not become her.

"Come on," I tell Hillary once she's maneuvered out of her boots. "My room."

I leave my bedroom door open, as per my parents' rules. In one of their rare moments of solidarity, they informed me that if I were straight, they wouldn't let me alone behind closed doors with a boy, even if I insisted he was only a friend, so the same rules apply now for girls.

I tried to argue with them when the rule was first instituted, but I think I only hurt my cause. Apparently, telling your parents that it's not like you couldn't find other places to fool around if you really meant to does not make them more amenable to giving you privacy. I'm used to it now, but it was strange at first, to suddenly not be allowed privacy with Hillary. Like our friendship was no longer trustworthy. Which was hard, because for a while, I feared that it wasn't.

Hillary was the first person I came out to, and I did it on a whim. There's no manual for that conversation, no matter how much you search for one on the Internet. I'd known for a really long time that I just wasn't attracted to boys. Years. Ever since I hit puberty and all my friends started swooning over windswept-haired pop stars and muscle-bound athletes, and I kept finding my eyes drawn instead to their female counterparts. And, in seventh grade, my friend Cadence decided she was madly in love with our other friend Felix, at the same time I decided I was madly in love, too— with Cadence. Neither crush ever came to anything, but mine ended less painfully, since to this day, I've never told her.

I was scared, then, of what people might think if I told them I was attracted to girls. Scared Hillary would roll her eyes and say I just hadn't found a good guy yet. Or worse, that I was *going through a phase.* That's what my first girlfriend's parents told her when she came out. Her horror stories pushed me to the back of the closet. I had no idea how to even broach the subject with my family and friends. How to phrase it, how to even bring it up.

But one day, near the end of my sophomore year, Hillary was being insufferably worried about my perpetual singleness, and how I'd just turned down a guy who was "*soo* cute!" when he asked me out earlier in the week.

"I'm *fine*," I said exasperatedly, and just blurted it out. "I've kissed people, just none of them are guys."

"Oh," she said. Then her eyes got comically huge, and she said it again: *"Oh."*

"This, uh, isn't how I meant to tell you." I wanted to die on the spot. I still remember the feeling. That utter oh-shit-what've-I-done heart-racing panic. "Please don't be freaked out. It doesn't mean—nothing's different about our friend-ship; I didn't mean to be misleading, I swear. I just had no idea how to tell you. I didn't want you to . . . I don't know."

It was a lot for her to take in, I could tell by her expression. And I understood, of course. I could only imagine her flashing back to all the times we'd changed in front of each other or slept in the same bed or compared boobs. Wondering if I had banked away those images for myself, or if I hadn't ever been into her, and if not, was something wrong with her? She may not have thought any of these things, but I had answers prepared for any part of it.

But whatever she thought in those first moments, she kept it to herself. She just hugged me and said, "So you're saying you've been kissing girls for a while now, and you've had *no one* to talk about it with?"

"I . . . I guess. A couple years. Yeah."

She pulled away from me and shook her head. "Well. I'm glad you told me now."

She smiled and I smiled and I cried a whole lot, relieved I'd done it, relieved it turned out okay. She asked me about my first kiss, and I told her all about it—a girl I'd met at overnight camp the summer before my freshman year who, I suppose, was the *actual* first person I ever came out to, though

I knew I'd never see her again after that, so in my head, it's not as significant. Especially since she came out to me first. It was near the end of the week when it happened, but two nights of sneaking out of our respective cabins to make out in the woods were enough to cement it for me: I was one hundred percent interested in girls, and girls only.

Hillary was so perfectly supportive that day, sitting in her room, listening to me go on about my first kiss. And then she broached the subject of her and me.

"Have you ever . . . I mean, you and I have been friends a long time. Do you . . . never mind."

"You want to know if I've ever had feelings for you?" I guessed. I knew it was coming.

"Well, I . . . yeah. I'm just curious."

"I don't want you to get offended," I said carefully. "But . . . no. Not because you're not, you know, pretty and stuff, just by the time I figured out how I felt, you and I had already been best friends for so long. I just couldn't see you that way."

"I'm not offended," she said. "Don't be silly. I just thought, if you *did* have feelings for me like that, we'd have to . . . deal with it, right?"

We had a little bit of an awkward period for a couple weeks after that; we didn't quite know how to interact with each other with my secret out in the open. She was careful not to touch me, even casually, like she didn't *quite* trust that I had no romantic feelings for her. But if you're a true friend, you don't stop loving someone because of something like this, and Hillary is a true friend, for sure.

Things were easier after that. It doesn't matter who you're

attracted to, it still helps to be able to tell your best friend about your crushes and your kisses and the first time you have sex. She helped me come out to the rest of our friends, stood beside me during the scary period when it started to go around school. She was there, months later, when I told my parents. My limbs felt like jelly, but having my best friend sitting beside me, I knew I could do it.

She was fierce: protective when the inevitable assholes started calling me names, undeterred when they started aiming their vitriol at her, too. People slipped nasty notes into my locker—occasionally, they still do—and one girl made a horrible scene in the locker room before gym class that left me in tears.

But I'm lucky; I have the absolute greatest friends, and they saw me through those tougher times. For all that things changed when I came out, they also stayed surprisingly the same.

Hillary plops into my desk chair, her seat of choice in my room since I first got a computer desk in sixth grade, and I onto my bed. She swivels toward me partway and props her legs up on my bookshelf.

"So, have a good day with Aracely?" she asks, grinning.

"Quiet! My mom thinks I was here." I lower my voice. "And it was good. Kind of great, actually. Is that fucked up?"

"No way. Not at all. I mean, *everything* doesn't have to suck just because the planet is being a huge asshole."

I snort. "The planet is being an asshole?"

"I don't think there's any question about that. First blood, now hair. And who knows what might come next."

All sorts of things come to mind. Horrible things. Flesh

or skin or worse. The revulsion inside of me manifests as a shiver. I think about my nightmares and then shove them back into the mind-corner where they belong.

"Did I miss anything at school?" I ask quickly, because I can tell by her face that she doesn't want to think about this any more than I do.

"Not really. Mikayla got mad at Cadence as usual, but she was over it by lunch. And this morning the principal gave a weird speech about not losing focus on our studies even during this"—she pauses to make air quotes—"'time of change.'"

"'Time of change,'" I repeat in monotone. "What is his problem?"

Hillary shrugs. "Oh, and evidently prom planning is on hold, too. Because if this doesn't stop, we're not having it, I guess."

"What? That's crap. What do we do if it goes away and prom arrives and it's just a glorified dance because we gave up planning for it?"

I haven't decided what I'm doing, personally, about prom yet. When I went in to order my family members' graduation tickets, the principal made it very clear—without stating outright—that I was both welcomed and encouraged to go to prom with whoever I'd like. *Whoever*, wink, wink. I appreciated the conversation, despite the fact that he seriously did wink, because while I've had fairly minimal drama at school over my sexuality—outside of the handful of expected bigoted jerks—our area is conservative, and part of me worried I might cause one of those situations where everyone has to take a stand on my behalf.

But even if my potential prom date is principal-approved, I don't know that Aracely will be ready to come out before prom. And the last thing I want to do is pressure her.

But still. It's prom. I can't imagine it cancelled, whether I go with a date or not.

"I know." Hillary pushes on the spine of a book with her toes. "It's dumb. Screw the apocalypse."

"Screw the bloodpocalypse," I amend enthusiastically, but then it kind of seems wrong to joke about it.

It's hard to believe it's only been a week since Hillary and I first saw blood in the cemetery. And it's hard to believe how quickly everything can change.

"Girls." Mom knocks on my open door. "Lea's stew looks ready. Also, the president is about to give an address, if you're interested."

We are definitely interested. The president has given addresses about this every night so far, each speech barely adding information to the last. But I keep hoping eventually he'll say something that matters.

The three of us sit on the couch with our bowls of stew while we wait through the typical pre-address speculation by the newscasters.

The president looks drawn, tired, older. He's dealt with a lot in his term—hurricanes and school shootings and more—but none of that could ever have prepared him for this.

He glances down at the papers before him—his script-writer-crafted speech—then picks them up and sets them upside-down with a curt efficiency.

"We don't know what's happening," he begins. "I won't continue to mislead you by pretending we do. This event is unprecedented. Here is what we know: a blood-like substance covers most of the earth's surface, now with what appears to be human hair mixed in. The greatest scientific minds from around the world are at work on finding answers, but in the meantime, I must emphasize that you stay calm. One positive thing that we *do* know is this: the substance is not hurting us. It has been tested extensively for blood-borne pathogens and other toxins, and none have been found. You are of course encouraged to be diligent, but any outbreaks of illness that may occur during this time are purely coincidental, so there is no need for panic."

He goes on to advise about emergency preparedness and government agencies on standby for disaster relief and the importance of staying calm and united during these uncertain times. He talks about the concerns people have about the blood permeating our water system, and assures us that for the time being, water is still drinkable after the use of filtration devices, and that emergency caches are being set up across the nation where safe drinking water will be flown in for those having a hard time getting a supply for themselves.

"So our water is affected now?" Hillary looks concerned.

"Is it, Mom?" I ask. I should've seen this coming, after what Dad said. But I didn't, somehow.

"I don't know. Haven't used any since this morning."

I go to the kitchen and grab the sink handle, hesitating. Do I want to see what comes out of here? Hillary and Mom crowd behind me, waiting, so there's not much choice.

I lift the handle and water flows out. Just water.

Anticlimactic, but a relief. I don't really want to drink water with blood in it, even after it's been filtered. Just because the president says it's safe doesn't mean it's true. He says untrue things all the time.

"Guess ours is fine still." Mom smiles brightly. "Maybe this'll all blow over before we have to worry about it."

I resist rolling my eyes. Yeah, because this could possibly just *blow over*.

The still-running sink coughs, and the water turns pinkish. Barely a blush, but enough that I can tell it's not just water anymore. I shut it off.

Mom frowns at the sink.

"I should go home," Hillary says. Her voice wavers. "See you tomorrow?"

"Definitely." I say it firmly because I feel Mom's eyes digging holes into me. "Unless they cancel school."

Hillary leaves with the hunched posture of a person crippled by worry.

"What happens now?" I ask Mom.

"We start filtering our water," she answers in a falsely cheery voice. "Good thing I ordered Brita filters in bulk last time!"

Ugh. I haven't even had any, and already my tongue feels heavy and metallic. I watch Mom fill our Brita pitcher with a growing dread. The pink-tinged water drips from the filter, slightly less pink, but still decidedly not clear. No. Fuck no.

"Mom, I am *not* drinking that."

Her eyes snap to mine. "You have to."

"I don't . . . I can't—*no*." I can't even articulate, I'm just, I'm *horrified*. Panicked. My heart claws at my throat with razor-sharp barbs. I feel like I have to escape, but there's nowhere to escape to.

"Lea, we have to drink water." Mom looks at me like I've lost it.

"We have other water. From before. I can't, *we* can't drink water with blood in it."

"Sweetheart." Mom reaches out to touch my cheek. "The president says—"

"I don't *care* what he says!" My voice is rising hysterically, and I know it makes me sound unreasonable, but fuck. She's acting like this is nothing. Like it's just fluoride or something, meant to be there. "Has *he* drank any, do you think? He's just saying shit; he wants us to stay calm. But maybe we shouldn't *be* calm."

Mom's hands shake as she replaces the pitcher in the fridge. "Lea. We will not panic until it is time to panic. That time has not come."

For a moment, I empathize with her. There's fear behind her eyes. She doesn't like this, either, but she's the parent and I'm the kid. She has to pretend she's fine so I believe it, so I feel safe. Maybe, now, I can do the same for her. I will my body to relax despite the rod of fear that tightens my spine, and I take a deep breath to free the knot in my chest as best I can.

"I won't panic," I say in the calmest possible voice. "Just don't make me drink that water quite yet."

Mom envelops me in a tight hug. My mother is not a small woman. Hugging her is like hugging a soft pillow, one with the comforting scent of home. But right now, it feels like the pillow is suffocating me. And the scent of home is dulled because scrubbing with a washcloth in front of the sink is not as effective as actually showering. Will we even be able to do that again?

"Everything's going to be all right. Your father and I will keep you safe from this," she says firmly. "Okay?"

I just nod. I appreciate the sentiment, but I'm not sure how she thinks she could protect me.

Our water is turning pink. The streets are filled with blood and hair. This is what it looks like when a world dies.

7.

Our teachers are trying to pretend like nothing strange is happening outside. I wonder if it was a conscious decision—one where they all gathered and talked it over during the week school was closed—or if they're hoping it will stop being real.

But it's clearly on their minds. It slips into our classwork. In biology, we forego AP practice exams and instead talk about how corpses progress through decomposition. In psych, we learn about the psychological trauma residents of disaster zones often face. This is a much less disgusting topic, but it kind of depresses me.

Lunch, right before third period, is a relief. Lunch is familiar. We have the same assortment of sandwiches and burgers, soggy fries, wilted salads, semi-bruised fruits, and single-gulp-sized containers of juice and milk as ever. Two water coolers sit at the end of the lunch line, bubbling happily as people fill plastic cups with clear, uncontaminated liquid. I've barely had any at home because even drinking from our older water supply makes me gag. Greedily, I take two cups, draining one before I've even left the lunch line.

I find my friends at our usual corner table. It's easier to sit in the corner—people aren't always tripping over your chair legs or smacking you in the back of the head with their trays. I appear to be the last one here today, unless Mikayla decides to sit with us. But no, I spy her a few tables away. She meets my gaze for a second, then turns away haughtily. It's not a surprise. She becomes inexplicably mad at one of us at least weekly. And when she's mad at one of us, she's mad at all of us. It used to get her all kinds of attention, but ever since we figured out that that was the point, we've stopped enabling it so much.

I sit next to Hillary, who appears to have invited Levi to join us today. Which is new. He eyes me warily, as usual, but seems to decide our friend Felix is a bigger threat, and turns his attention that way.

I don't trust Levi, I decide. If you think everyone your girlfriend associates with is a potential threat to your claim, there's something off about you.

"The French fries looked so effing good today," says Cadence, waving one toward my face. It does seem to have a little more structural integrity than usual, but just looking at it makes my stomach feel slick with grease.

"Ew," I say, fending off the fry with a plastic knife.

Cadence just shrugs, combs her fingers through her dyed-red hair, and pops the fry into her mouth. She is the sort of girl other girls are jealous of because she has this flawless, effortless edge to her. When Hillary and I got our lip piercings, we were self-conscious for weeks. Whenever I walked by a group of people laughing, I had this irrational paranoia that they were talking about how I couldn't pull it off. But Cadence, she can pull off *any* look, and she knows it. She is a presence, and I both envy and love that about her.

But she's not the only one whose presence is magnetizing. Aracely sits on the other side of the cafeteria, laughing with her friends. She's comparing rain boots with one of them, and I'm reminded of her extensive shoe collection. She usually never wears the same pair twice in one week. This must be killing her.

She catches me watching her. Our eyes meet, and a hint of a smile touches her lips. I return the expression, but only for a second, because then I have to dodge an orange flying at my head.

"Hey!" I protest, picking up the orange from where it landed on the floor.

Felix grins. He's fairly average looking most of the time, but he's got the most beautiful, dimpled smile. "You weren't listening. We're betting how long till the blood's gone."

I hold out the orange on my palm. "Can I bet never?"

Wrong bet. Felix takes his orange back gently and frowns at his plate. "Never mind."

"No, I'm sorry. I was only joking. It can't last forever, right?"

We lapse into silence. Cadence uses her last French fry to smear ketchup into smooth lines across the bottom of her fry container. Felix starts peeling his orange. Levi bites into an apple with a crisp *crunch*. He hasn't said a word during all of lunch, I realize. He's been dating Hillary for long enough now that he should be able to at least make small talk with us. I don't know if I've ever had a real conversation with him. And I can't think of anything to say to start one up.

It's too awkward, sitting here like a bunch of people who don't even know each other.

"So who is Mikayla pissed at today?" I ask, turning the subject away. She's the electron furthest from our nucleus. The one that is most easily lured to other atoms. We've been friends since grade school, but I know without a doubt that she's the first one I'll lose touch with when I head down-state to UNH for college in the fall. It doesn't bother me too much, but it bothers Hillary. She wants us all to be as devoted to her friends-first notion as she is, to put our everything into it despite Mikayla's hot-and-coldness, but sometimes it just doesn't work that way. Some friendships are meant to be temporary.

"Who even knows," says Hillary. "She was perfectly normal with me during French."

"Oh, it's me this time," says Felix, not looking a bit abashed. "I made a joke about peaches, and she didn't think it was funny."

"What kind of joke?" asks Cadence.

"Like you can't guess." I laugh.

Felix grins proudly. "It's not my fault if my sense of humor is too advanced."

"I'm sorry, but your humor is actually, like, first-grade level," Cadence says.

Felix squeezes his orange at her, and she squeals. Levi is staring at the clock like he's counting the seconds. Irritation flashes through me. He should appreciate this more. He gets to sit with his girlfriend at lunch and it's just . . . normal. Expected. He's not making any statement about himself, not creating any gossip, not losing any friends. If Aracely sat with us, she would be talking to everyone right now, getting to know them, not frowning at her plate.

I glance over at her again. Would she lose friends, if she came out? I don't know any of them well enough to guess. I hope they would stand by her, but I'm not naïve enough to think none of them would drift away, whether they did it consciously or not. It happened to me. Though if someone can't care about you for who you are, how good of a friend are they anyway? I don't miss the ones who drifted.

"So hey, Lea," Cadence redirects my attention. "Where were you yesterday?"

"I was with—I was at home." I mentally flinch at my near slipup. They've never seen Aracely and me together. There's no reason for us to be hanging out. Besides the obvious. If I'd said her name, they'd already be grilling me for relationship details, and by the end of the day, half the school would know about Aracely. Because Felix cannot keep a secret to save his life, as I learned the hard way—several times—in middle school.

"You were home with . . . ," prompts Felix. He is, unfortunately, as shrewd as he is loudmouthed.

Hillary and I exchange a nervous look.

"My mom. She wasn't feeling well."

"From the blood?" Cadence leans away from me like I'm infected.

"What? No. Migraine. Don't be dumb. They've said like a billion times on the news that the blood isn't toxic."

"Yeah, and they also said it wasn't blood, so excuse me if I'm skeptical."

I tear the wrapper from my burger to shreds. "Fair point, I guess. But really, it was just a migraine."

"My sister told me some girl at her college had, like, a full-on mental breakdown from it," Cadence says.

She's really not letting this go. I'm torn between curiosity and a desire to get us way, way off this topic.

Hillary spares me the decision, asking, "What happened?"

"Apparently she just started screaming in the middle of campus and painted herself with blood. All over her face and her arms and everything. My sister saw the whole thing. They had to take her to the hospital."

"Wow." Felix squeezes one of his orange slices slowly, making a puddle on his plate. "Maybe she was already, you know, on the brink. And this was too much for her."

"Maybe," Cadence says, but I can tell she doesn't believe it. Her eyes flick to me again, and I resist the urge to scream that it was *just a fucking migraine* because it's not even real.

The bell rings—a relief—and we dump our trays. Hillary and I have English now, but I'm sort of hoping to cross paths with Aracely, even if only for a second. I hang back as we are spit out the other side of the bottleneck in the cafeteria doorway. Aracely's at the trash. So close by, and she definitely sees me.

But Hillary tugs hard on my arm, dragging me off toward the stairs.

"You should've included Levi more in our conversation at lunch," she says.

Oh, for the love.

"*I* should have? He's not my boyfriend. Besides, he didn't even say hi when I sat down. That's on him."

"You didn't say hi, either."

"Yeah, well, I usually don't say hi to people who are glaring at me."

We're almost to English, but she stops me, a sharp frown on her face. "You don't like him, do you?"

"I . . . I don't hate him or anything. He's just, I don't know. He's wicked possessive of you. Jealous of me and of Felix. And I don't like *that*."

"Seriously?" She crosses her arms roughly. "Possessive?

Anytime I tell him I'm doing something with you guys, without him, he says okay. Any. Time. So what if he's jealous of you. So fucking what. You should be flattered. He obviously thinks you're pretty enough to lure me over or whatever."

My temper flares. "Yeah because that's all it takes. Obviously, I can change your sexuality if I smile the right way, because it's that easy."

"Jesus Christ, Lea. That's not what I meant and you know it. Don't even make this about you right now. You just admitted you don't like my boyfriend and—" She cuts off because we're starting to draw questioning glances from others in the hall. In a lowered voice, she continues, "I don't know what to do if you don't like him."

The expression on her face is so pitiful, it grabs my heart and wrenches. "I'm sorry, Hill. I'll try harder, okay? I swear, it's not that I hate him, I'm just protective of you. I never trust your boyfriends until I get to know them better."

She tilts her head, brows pulled together slightly, like she's trying to decide if I'm being honest.

"Well." She sighs. "I do understand *that*."

"Good." I smile at her.

She smiles back, and gives me a quick hug. The familiar scent of her floral perfume is like a burst of color in the gray-tiled hallway. I consider making a joke about what Levi would think if he saw us hugging, but maybe I shouldn't rock the boat two seconds after our fight ended.

"Now let's go talk about some stories we didn't read, huh?"

I laugh and wave my absence excuse form at her. "Well, since I was just so ill yesterday, I think I'm excused."

"Oh my God." She snatches it. "You did not seriously get your mom to write a note that you were sick."

"I sure did."

"I hate you." She hands me back my slip with an expression of faux disgust.

Our English teacher, Mr. Hannard, initials my slip without even glancing at it and hands me a stapled stack of copied pages. I glance at it on the way to my seat. Edgar Allan Poe. We've been doing short stories for the past couple weeks, so he was bound to come up. But he's so morbid. I'm growing even more suspicious that the teachers actively decided to be disturbing this week.

I have high hopes for today's class, though. Mr. Hannard can be a little dry, but it seems like Edgar Allan Poe's creepy-awesomeness should negate that.

Or not. Five minutes in, I figure I could be hearing a lecture on how to put wood through a chipper, and it'd be just as interesting.

I draw a heart on the corner of my notebook in homage to "The Tell-Tale Heart" (and also because I'm bored). But somehow it ends up with Aracely's initials in it, and when I think about what a sinister story it is, I scribble out the heart.

As we start "The Raven," I stare at the drawn curtains over our classroom windows and wonder where all the real ravens have gone. What they're eating. If they're dying. I've been so wrapped up in my own horror the past couple days, I haven't thought about the animals at all. I can't recall seeing any. Or hearing any. The world has gone silent. There's a stillness over everything, like that moment when winter's first blanket of snow settles over the ground.

Except this is a different kind of stillness. It doesn't feel like tranquility; it feels like a tomb.

"Quoth the raven, 'Nevermore,'" this poem says, repeatedly.

And I know Edgar Allan Poe's message is an entirely different one, but I can't help but think: how tremendously fitting.

8.

Cadence and I have last period free on Tuesdays and Thursdays. And since we're seniors, we're allowed to leave during it.

"What should we do?" she asks me. "I don't feel like going home yet."

I'm not surprised. Cadence never feels like going home.

"Bookstore?" I suggest. "The sky doesn't look great."

I didn't think to look at the weather forecast this morning. I just figured it was bloody with a chance of hair. And when I left the house, the sun was beaming in full force. But now, dark clouds sit plumply overhead, and I suspect rain is imminent. Maybe I should've brought some soap. I might finally get a shower.

"Sure," she says. "We can get started on our homework. Maybe."

It's impossible to walk quickly down the hill, since we're traveling with a river of blood and a slippery mat of hair. I wonder how the blood keeps streaming like this. Isn't it eventually just going to fill everything up?

Maybe that's the plan here. The earth's plan. It's going to fill all the valleys like big bowls of tomato soup, and leave us all crowding desperately on mountaintops, fighting not to fall in.

We reach the bottom of the hill just as it begins to rain.

"Dammit!" Cadence shields her hair ineffectively with her hands. "Let's go to the library instead."

The library is much closer, just down the sidewalk. A flat sidewalk now that we're off the hill, though the blood is significantly deeper here. Only a couple inches below the tops of my boots. I shuffle carefully so I don't slosh any inside.

There aren't a whole lot of other people out here. There's tons of road traffic, but this part of town is filled with cute shops and restaurants and the movie theater, and right now people are only interested in shopping for essentials. Those who *are* out are tense and electric, and now that it's raining, there's a palpable desperation in the air as everyone rushes for sanctuary.

There's something not quite right about this rain. I slow, holding out my hand to let the droplets fall on my palm.

The liquid isn't clear. It's hard to tell exactly what color it is because it's fairly translucent, but I know anyway.

Red.

There's blood in the rain.

Cut into the lawn in front of the library is a long set of stone steps, because the building is set back a bit from the road. And at the base of the steps stands a man wearing long, white robes. The hem dips below the surface of the blood, and the fabric has absorbed liquid. It creeps up and up, and I have this mental image of the blood creeping all the way to his head and enveloping him and slowly melting back down to the ground.

He's reading from a Bible so big, he has to hold it with both hands. If I had any doubt about the rain, it's gone now. Pink splotches speckle the shoulders of his robes: macabre polka dots.

Cadence pushes past him, and I mean to follow her, but I'm entranced.

Blood drips from the beige leather cover of the man's

Bible as he shouts passages from the book. It's like the words of God are leaking through the pages in the form of bloody tears.

"'And God said unto Noah!'" The man practically screams this into my face. I flinch, but can't back away. His voice is hoarse with overuse and passion. "'The end of all flesh is come before me; for the earth is filled with violence through them; and behold, I will destroy them with the earth.'"

I shiver. Not from the pink-tinged rain that's splashing onto my shoulders, but from the quote, which slides over my skin like a chill.

"Come *on*, Lea!" Cadence shouts. "What are you doing?"

She breaks me from my trance. "Sorry! I'm coming."

We rush up the rest of the steps, yank open the excessively heavy door, and collapse inside the library. The librarian barely looks up from behind her desk, but we barely look at her, either.

"Blood is falling from the sky," says Cadence.

We're sitting side by side on a wooden bench near the door, shell-shocked and shivering.

"It sure is."

She stares me squarely in the eye. There are three freckles on her nose. I've never noticed them before.

"We're doomed."

Hillary picks us up after school lets out. She's a godsend with an enormous umbrella, and she parks in the lot behind the library so we don't have to run down to the street.

"You guys are idiots," she says. "Didn't you figure it'd rain? The sky was, like, black."

"Yeah." Cadence squeezes her hair even though it's no longer damp. "*Water*. Raining blood isn't possible."

"None of this is possible." Hillary grips the steering wheel of her Chevy Cobalt with white-knuckled fists. "Do you *see* what I'm driving through?"

Her car is parting an ocean of red. I see her point. But Cadence slumps in the backseat with a sigh. I tap my fingers on the seat, feeling awkward.

"How's your brother doing?" I ask Hillary to break the tension.

"Finn's okay. He's had some nightmares and stuff and he's, like, full-on physically attached to whatever older person's nearest, but I think he could be handling it a lot worse."

Hillary's forehead creases when she talks about her brother, the way it always does when she's concerned about someone's well-being. She wants to go to school for social work, and I cannot imagine anyone more suited to the career than Hillary and her three-sizes-too-large heart.

"He'll be okay," Cadence says, threading her fingers through the damp strands of her hair. "He's got you."

We turn into my driveway, and my gut knots at the idea of going back into the rain.

"Thanks, Hill," I say. Then, to both, "Text me!"

I run inside as quickly as possible, mostly avoiding further pelting by the blood-rain. On my way, I step on something that crunches, but it could be anything—no way I'm stopping to look.

My house greets me with a burst of warmth. I hadn't noticed the chill outdoors; I was just focused on the rain. I slip out of my boots and make directly for my room to change out of this blood-spattered outfit.

"Mom?" I call when I've wiped my skin clean with a towel and pulled on some pj pants and a tank top. It's after four o'clock; she should be home.

In answer, she emerges from the basement, behind a door at the end of the hall. She looks pale and tired and holds a book in one hand, though with the way her body's angled, I can't see what book it is.

"Oh, hey. So you *are* home. Did you see that it's raining?" I say, when she stops in front of me.

"Yes, I saw." She closes the door behind her, then glances between it and me. And in a dull, monotone voice, she says, "Don't go into the basement."

9.

I know that when a person says something like *don't go into the basement*, you should listen to them. Not listening to logical warnings is exactly how people get themselves killed in horror movies. And I don't want to be That Person in the horror movie that is my life. It's silly I'm even having this discussion with myself, really. I never go into the basement. It's just a boring square of cement with a washer and dryer and a bunch of storage bins. But now that Mom told me not to—and said it in that chilling voice—I am dying to go down there. Just for a second. Just to see.

I hear the scripted laughter of a sitcom audience drifting from the living room, and I grab my chance. On tiptoe, I creep out of my room and down to the far end of the hall, where the basement door is opposite my parents'. It opens with nothing but a whisper of faux wood scratching on carpet. I turn on the light and start my descent, pulling the door closed so Mom won't notice if she happens to glance down the hall.

Bloody footprints mar the surface of the pale, unvarnished maple steps. I avoid them, because I don't want to stain my socks, and I stop on the bottom stair because unless I'd like the socks to be scarlet, I can't go any farther.

I can't tell how deep it is—maybe an inch or two—but blood has seeped into our basement and it's settled thickly across the entire floor. It's obvious where it's come in from, because the cement walls are stained with rust-red waterfalls in several spots. Mom must have come down for something in one of the storage bins, because they look in disarray, with streaks of crimson up the sides of some. My stomach turns.

The blood is coming indoors now.

I had thought of indoors as a sanctuary. A place where we're free of the chaos. All our cement and wood and plaster, it's all for nothing. Not once has our basement ever flooded, and now it looks like a sick pit of murder.

A car door slams. Dad's home. I tiptoe hurriedly back up the steps, slip into the hallway, and press the door closed behind me. But I don't want to go in the kitchen or the living room while my parents sit together like strangers, so I close myself in my room and text Aracely instead.

I should have texted her earlier to see if she wanted a ride from Hillary, too.

But then Cadence would know and she would tell Felix, and even though she'd make him swear to secrecy, he'd tell the whole baseball team and . . . we're here again.

Aracely texts back that her dad picked her up, and she had a raincoat, anyway, so she was fine.

We end up chatting online. There's not much else to do, after all.

Me: *What do u think it means that it's raining blood?*

Her: *Idk. It doesn't make sense, right? Blood's too thick to evaporate.*

Aracely's better at science than me. I don't hate it as much as Hillary does, but I prefer the humanities. Aracely wants to be a chemist when she grows up. If this happened twenty years into the future instead of now, I wonder if she would be among the scientists trying to solve it all.

Me: *Maybe that means it's really not blood.*

Her: *Possibly . . . seems unlikely tho. I guess we'll hear some-*

thing if they figure it out.

I take this to mean she doesn't want to talk about that anymore.

Me: *Hey, sorry I didn't get to talk to u at school today.*

Her: *That's ok. At least we had yesterday :)*

Me: *Yesterday WAS pretty awesome.*

Her: *Two of my friends stayed home yesterday. They were pissed I didn't tell them I did too.*

Me: *You could've!*

Her: *You're too understanding. I didn't want to I wanted to hang out w you.*

Me: *:)*

Her: *Srsly. I love them but I need you too.*

She used the word *need*, and I know it doesn't really mean anything, but I am melting. It's not that I've had bad luck in romance. In fact, I'd say I've done okay. But there's something about the way Aracely says things, the way she focuses her attention on me when we're together, that makes me feel so *wanted*. She throws me off. She's much less experienced than me in every aspect of dating, but she's so open and straightforward, it makes me feel brand-new. Like I'm rediscovering my entire identity. I don't even know what to say to her right now.

Her: *Sorry. Need was a bad word, wasn't it?*

Me: *No! I liked it.*

Her: *:) :)*

Her: *Oh crap my dad's calling me, have to go.*

Me: *Ok. See u tomorrow, I hope.*

Her: *I hope too.*

I am grinning ear to ear. My cheeks hurt, but I cannot

make my face do anything else because just this tiny little online conversation was like a shot of pure joy straight into my chest. I want to sit here all night and think about seeing her tomorrow, and maybe we'll walk really near each other and our hands will brush and . . .

I comb my fingers through my hair. It's not too greasy yet—today's only the second day I haven't washed it at *all*—but it's a little crunchy in spots. Dried blood from the rain. My fingers tremble, my high diminishes a tiny bit. This is the first time I've actually gotten the blood *on* me. It's unsettling, to say the least. Where—or who—is this stuff from? The scientists on the news all agree that it's impossible for the earth to bleed, but they also now agree that that's exactly what is happening. It's been tested—all of it: the blood and the hair—and declared human. They've even supposedly found some intact DNA, but it's all intermixed, and trying to figure out who any of it might have come from was deemed not a good use of resources. Which makes sense to me, I guess. But knowing it's human isn't enough. We still don't know how it's coming up out of the ground like this, don't know how it's in the condition it's in, or why any of this is happening.

We don't know what to do to make it stop. Or, though no one ever says it outright, how we'll survive long-term if it doesn't. They're still insisting that it won't hurt us, but I remember Cadence's story from earlier about the girl on her sister's campus, and I'm worried.

I kneel on my bed, nose squished against the cool glass of my window. The night is black; I see nothing but a hint of the half-full moon. And I hear nothing but the dripping of rain from the eaves. It's deceptively soothing. The moon, the rain. They're familiar and ever-present. Relatable to people across the globe, whether they're in a tiny rural town like mine or a dangerous city in a war-torn nation on the other side of the earth.

We've fought so many wars in this world. Buried so many corpses. It's unfathomable, the number of people who have died since the dawn of time, whether at the end of long lives, or gone too soon. Some of them sent off with burials or rituals or cremation, others unceremoniously or worse. Is that where it's coming from? The blood of the injured left on battle-fields? The blood of our dead, drawn from their corpses?

Once, I saw a picture of someplace where so much violence had happened, the streets were literally running with blood. It made me feel sick and horrible; I wanted to rescue the innocents, even though I knew there was nothing I could do. And now, that's everywhere, only this time we don't know why.

I touch my hair again. It's death. There's death in my hair.

I grab my brush from my desk and rake it through my hair over and over. It's not doing anything, though. It might be pulling off some of the blood, but most of it is still on there. I throw the brush, and a half-sob type of noise bursts from my throat. My chest is heavy with intense but indescribable emotion. I just, I need to wash my hair. That's all I know.

It's time to brave the living room.

My parents sit on opposite sides of the couch, watching the news, as usual. The president again. He looks older, less certain of himself, every time I see him. My confidence is not inspired.

"Hey, Dad." I sit between my parents. Mom puts her arm

over a book that sits beside her, shoving it onto the end table out of sight. "So, which of the buckets are we using for, like, washing our hair and stuff?"

Both of them stare at me like I just asked where we store our stash of diamonds.

"Was that a joke?" Dad asks.

"No. There's dried blood in my hair from the rain and I have to go to school tomorrow, so I thought . . ." I trail off because judging by Dad's expression, only bad things can come from me finishing my sentence.

"Which do you think is more important, impressing your girlfriend or having water to drink?" Dad asks gruffly.

I know he wants me to say *water to drink*, but I think he's being unreasonable. It isn't about impressing anyone, it's about not feeling like there's a layer of gore pasted to my skin. One bucket of water to wash my hair so I don't feel so . . . *wrong*. That's all I'm asking for. *One.* I bet Aracely's dad is letting her wash her hair. There is *other people's blood* on me, and Dad's saying I can't clean it off? My stomach knots, almost painfully.

I say nothing.

"Your hair looks fine," Mom says.

That's how she takes Dad's side without openly doing so.

"Whatever."

"Don't *whatever* us, Lea," Dad warns. "This isn't a game. It's real life."

"I *know*. But there's millions of bottles of water out there, and I'm *sure* they're figuring this out and—"

"Who's they?" Dad interrupts.

"The government or scientists or whoever."

Mom's not even listening to me anymore. She's throwing away the paper plate from Dad's dinner, like it couldn't wait another second. And Dad's got his attention half on me, half on the president's stupid, pointless speech. Because we all know no one's figuring out anything, and my argument has no merit. But now I can't stop thinking about my hair. We're taught always, *always*, not to touch other people's blood. I want to shave my head to get rid of it.

"Never mind," I say, to neither in particular. "You don't get it."

"We do, sweetheart." Dad tears himself away from the TV. "But that doesn't change the reality."

"Sure."

I leave. I shouldn't have come out of my room in the first place. How could I have thought they'd understand? Neither of them has tried to attract anyone in a long, long time. And neither of them got caught unawares in a rainstorm of blood.

The thing is, I *do* understand their perspective. I know perfectly well that eventually, water might become unusable, and we will need to save what we have. But if they think water from our Brita filter is okay to *drink*, then why can't I wash with it? I'm already not washing my dirty clothes, which isn't a big deal yet, but it will be. And Mom got me like thirty pairs of the most unsexy underwear I've ever seen, which tells me they are very serious about no laundry. I'm just not to re-wear anything that gets bloodstained. But I guess that doesn't apply to my body. And why not?

I brush my hair again, and think of the crazy man from earlier. The way the blood crawled up his robes and dripped off his Bible. And I think of the quote he screamed in my face. I want to read more of it. Which is a weird feeling.

I'm not much of a religious person. My dad's family are lapsed Methodists, and my mom is firmly atheist after a childhood living with parents who were part of what probably qualifies as a religious cult. None of my grandparents are still alive, but both sets gifted me Bibles at some point during my youth. The Bibles have just been collecting dust ever since. I pull out the one I like more—it has a velvety cover and one of those attached ribbon bookmarks—and search for the story of Noah. I'm pretty sure it's in Genesis, but Genesis is huge and harder to skim through than you might think.

I never went to Bible school or anything, so I don't know where to begin. My parents haven't stopped me from religious exploration, but Mom discouraged it in subtle ways throughout my childhood. She was pretty traumatized by the severity of her upbringing, and likes to point out the uselessness of faith whenever possible. Just yesterday, she scoffed at a news story about people trying to get to religious centers like Vatican City and Mecca, despite the current ban on air travel. "Waste of time," she said. "If anything proves there's no God, it's this."

A knock on my door startles me. "Honey?" Mom calls softly.

"What?" I stow the Bible quickly under my pillow.

She comes in. "I brought you something."

It's our small mixing bowl, full of water.

"I'm not thirsty."

"No, it's—" She glances over her shoulder, even though she closed the door, and lowers her voice. "It's for your hair. I know it's not much, but . . ."

I dart up from my bed and take it before she changes her mind. "I thought you agreed with Dad on this one."

"Well . . . I do. He's absolutely right that we shouldn't be wasting water. But you're right, too. You should be allowed cleanliness. Just this once, I think it'll be okay."

I set the bowl on my desk and hug her tightly. "Thanks, Mom."

"I understand, you know." She pulls back, holding me by the shoulders with a smile. "I was a teenager once. It's hard to be young. I don't want it to be hard for you; I don't want . . . this."

She touches my cheek. Her eyes have a gloss, which brings a lump to my throat. My parents do try their best to make my life easy, and I'm grateful for that. Though maybe, sometimes, not grateful enough.

"Love you, Mom."

She smiles again. "Love you, too, sweetheart."

She leaves me alone with my water and my Bible. While I figure out how best to utilize what little water I've been given, I take the Bible back out and skim through it again until I find Noah and his ark. Considering how much has been made of this particular tale over the years, it's not a very long one.

I shut the Bible, frowning. Well, if there *is* a God, and he really did all the stuff in here, then either he's not responsible for this, or he's a liar because he promises emphatically that after the floods end, he won't ever destroy the earth like that again. I almost wish he'd promised the opposite.

Wouldn't it be easier if there was a God to blame? If he'd said to Noah, "So listen, I hope I never have to do this again, but if you humans can't get it together, I will flood you out no matter how many tries it takes to fix what you've all done wrong," then maybe there would be an explanation for what is happening right now.

I shove the Bible back where it belongs on my shelf. Its gold-lettered spine stares at me, and I realize what my mom tried to casually hide from me earlier—twice. What she went into the basement for. I'm not the only one who turned to religion for answers. My mom, the hypocrite, has gotten out her old Bible, the one she hasn't read in at least a decade.

I only hope she finds more answers in the pages of her Bible than I did in mine.

10.

It's creepy how we've adjusted to this new life. I guess that's the way of it. You adapt or you don't survive.

That's why I walk out of my house each morning with my chin lifted. Our entryway isn't hopelessly stained with blood if I don't look at it.

No one comments on the *slippery when wet* signs near all the entrances at school. We act like it's normal to sort of skate with our feet so we don't fall on the slick floor. Ignore the trickle of liquid that sloshes in when we open the door, and the janitor who has become a doorman with a mop.

Cars drive extra slowly so they don't splash unsuspecting pedestrians. We ignore news stories about subways flooding and cities shutting down because it's impossible for them to go on. We don't have to deal with that sort of thing out here in the middle of nowhere. We are stronger. We are different. That's what we want to believe.

And everything's all right, so long as we believe it.

Aracely meets me at the crosswalk, as usual, and wordlessly, we link arms. Bracing each other makes it less likely one of us will fall. This is one of the few benefits I've discovered over the days. Strangers and friends alike have started walking in pairs or in groups to combat the blood's tides, and the way the hair seems sometimes to reach out and grab you. Grocery stores may be practical war zones, but out here, on the streets, we support each other. We are chains of survival. And it means that Aracely and I can walk together, touching, and not an eyebrow is raised.

My feet are used to the matted cushion of hair beneath

the warm lake of blood. I'm cautious and prepared for clumps that might catch on my toes. It's routine.

But today.

Today we have to adapt again because the air is heavy with a horrible, horrible smell. A putrid, festering stink. In truth, the air always smells kind of bad these days, but it's grown worse. I nearly gag with each inhalation, and the air struggles through my lungs as though thick with humidity. I stub my toe on something hard that skitters away afterward, and if not for Aracely, I would now be facedown in the blood.

I always regret it when I look at the ground, but I look anyway.

The blood is different. Darker, sludgy. Like perhaps it's starting to rot. Breathing it feels like inhaling poison.

Something white arches up out of the murk, near my foot. Against my better judgment, I push my toes beneath it and lift.

It's a bone.

A rib bone, perfectly smooth and ivory except for the places where blood has been absorbed into small cracks in its structure.

Aracely stops dead. She eyes the door of her building, but I shake my head before she can suggest skipping. I would love nothing more than to go inside and forget that this night-mare exists, but I can't.

"I don't know about your dad, but my parents will ground me for the next freaking century if I skip again," I tell her.

"I know," Aracely says. "I know we have to go, I just . . ." She holds more tightly to my arm. "I'll be fine. Let's go."

We walk.

We walk slowly, picking our way through the obstacle course the streets have become. Once we reach School Street, we meet up with other walkers, and our chain of support grows. By the time we make it to the school, we probably look like a shambling army of zombies, come to tear flesh off apocalypse survivors.

I can barely breathe. I'm sucking air through my shirt, but even with the fabric over my mouth and nose, the stench is intolerable. Queasiness grips my stomach. One girl already hurled, and I'm determined not to be next. Tears sting my eyes—partly from the rawness of the stench, partly from the suffocating coat of fear that's painting itself thicker and thicker over my skin.

I've seen gross things before. Hillary and I went on a hunting trip once with Felix's family, back before his dad left. We had to help gut the deer. Entrails and blood everywhere. It steamed in the cool fall air and smelled of fresh death. The deer's tongue lolled out of its mouth, and its black, glassy eyes never closed. And I've seen bones. Once, half a cow skeleton inexplicably washed up at the beach near the dam where my dad works. The bones were cracked and weathered, but we all thought they were cool. Cadence and I had a sword fight with femurs while Hillary and Mikayla tried to pry a tooth from the skull.

But none of that compares to this invasive, consuming stench. To tripping and stumbling and slipping at every step. To not understanding anything about what's going on with our planet, not knowing how long we'll survive like this.

The janitor holds open the door as we all file through. He smiles grimly in response to my thanks, and goes to work mopping up our bloody tracks.

"Wow." Aracely exhales roughly, leaning against a locker.

"I know." I cough, my lungs forcibly exhaling what they can of the stench and the thickness.

"You all right?"

"Yeah, I'm fine."

One of the guys from our zombie chain barges between us. "Hey, that was some walk to school, huh?"

His eyes are on Aracely. He puts a hand on her shoulder. I pull my lip ring between my teeth to stop myself from telling him to go the hell away.

"Yeah, it sucked." She sidesteps, removing herself from his invasive touch.

"Next time, you should walk beside me. I'm very strong."

Gag.

"No thanks," she says coolly. Her posture, the look in her eyes, her tone, all radiate disinterest, but he doesn't seem to care.

He just shrugs and walks off with a flirty smirk.

Aracely rolls her eyes upward like she's praying for patience.

"God, I hate when they do that," she says.

I open my mouth to tell her there's an easy way to get boys to stop hitting on her, but then close it again. Because I'm wrong. When I first came out, I suddenly became fascinating to boys who'd never spoken to me before. Not *all* boys, of course, but the number who developed a suspiciously timed interest in me was not insignificant. Even now, I'll sometimes have a determined one try to "turn me straight." Or convince me of the merits of bisexuality, because their girlfriend is so hot, they swear, a threesome will be worth it.

Aracely would most definitely face all that crap, too, and I don't want her to have to if she's not ready.

Though if I'm honest with myself, I wish she was ready.

The school's intercom system crackles to life. "Attention all students and faculty." It's the vice principal's voice. "School has been cancelled for the day."

My first feeling is relief. My second, misery. I can't do that walk again. My lungs are still heavy with the air's putrid filth.

The vice principal continues, something about bus schedules and using caution if walking.

"They couldn't have made this decision forty minutes ago?" Aracely complains.

"No kidding."

My phone vibrates. A text from Hillary: *Want a ride home?*

YES. I'm near the front entrance, I text back, then look up at Aracely. "Do you want a ride home, from Hillary?"

"I . . ." She bites her lip. "I don't know. Maybe. Just the three of us?"

"I'm not sure. She'll be here in a sec. I can ask."

The question answers itself, because Hillary approaches with Levi in tow.

"I'm going to walk," says Aracely. "I'll see you, okay?"

"Wait, should I—"

"No. This is my problem. I'll be fine, I promise. Look, I can see my friend Marina."

And she's gone before I can say anything else. I'm torn. Not a fiber of my being wants to go back out into that mess, but I also feel like I'm betraying Aracely somehow. Choosing my selfish desire not to walk over staying with her.

But I invited her to come in the car. That's all I could do, right? She has friends of her own. I can't see if she actually found one of them or if she's lying, but either way, it was her decision.

Hillary reaches me, her fingers woven through Levi's. I wish he weren't here so I could ask her what she thinks I should have done.

"Hey, guys," I greet them both, and even manage a smile at Levi.

He smiles back, in a startled sort of way, and I feel bad. Do I never smile at him? What *does* my face usually look like when I see him? I don't think of myself as a mean person, but I guess I've been pretty cold toward him.

"What are your plans now that school's out?" Hillary asks.

"I don't know. I'm going to have to call my mom, probably."

"Wanna hang out with us?" Levi asks.

Hillary and I give him identical confused expressions, and he grins a wide, bleached-white smile.

"Everyone's parents will object less if it's the three of us, right?" he explains.

I laugh. "Clever."

"Don't let word get out." He winks at me. My feelings toward him cool, but then I mentally chastise myself. A wink doesn't have to be flirting. He's probably just being awkward. We're getting along, and I want to get along, and I'm not going to ruin it by being an asshole for no reason.

"Ready to go out there?" Hillary asks.

"I guess." I cover my mouth and nose with my shirt again,

and they do the same. We don't have far to walk, but we do still have to cross the parking lot.

Outside, I spot Aracely immediately. She *is* with her friend Marina. She looks happy enough, but as I watch her make her way down the hill, tears prick my eyes. I don't know how to keep her a secret while also spending enough time with her. Will I end up losing her? I don't want that. I feel like our relationship is sun-dried sand, falling through the cracks between my fingers. She's given no indication that this isn't working for her, but it scares me anyway.

"Are you okay?" Hillary grabs my elbow.

"Yes," I say, but it's creaky and uncertain.

She frowns. "Hey, Levi, I'm going to drop you off at your house, okay?"

His face darkens.

"You don't need to do that," I say, but my voice still has that weird hitch, even muffled as it is through my T-shirt. We make it to her car and I breathe a sigh of relief. It doesn't smell *good*, but it smells better.

Levi glowers at me from the front passenger seat, and I duck my head. What does he want from me? I'm not a saint. A weak protest is the most I can do, because alone time with my best friend is exactly what I wanted.

"It's fine," Levi says tightly.

And then no one says anything while Hillary pulls out of the lot and heads farther up the hill, toward Levi's house.

"You're sure?" Hillary breaks the silence finally, looking at him with her big, gray, pleading eyes.

His scowl softens into a smile as she pulls into his driveway. "Yes, I'm sure." He glances at me for the briefest moment before giving her a lingering kiss and getting out of the car.

As we pull away, he watches us, the expression on his face one I recognize well. He knew Hillary was like this from the start. She makes her commitment to her friends very clear, from the first date. Just like I knew Aracely and I would have to be a secret. But knowing it doesn't make living it any easier.

And in this moment, for the first time, I think maybe Levi and I have something in common after all.

Bones Found to Be of Human Origin, Blood Beginning to Fester

Bones began appearing beneath the blood late last night through early this morning, accompanied by a distinct change in the smell of the substance. Government scientists worldwide have been researching the situation, and have concluded that the bones appear of human origin.

"We're finding bones from all parts of the skeleton," said one researcher, who requested anonymity. "But they appear to be scattered at random. We have yet to find a cluster of bones that originated from one individual skeleton. Any animal bones that have been brought to research facilities appear to be older, and unrelated to our current situation."

In reference to the worsened smell of the blood, the researcher had this to say: "We are still checking further into possible underlying causes, but mainly, blood just cannot remain out in the sun for days without starting to rot."

As negative as this sounds, researchers say there is no reason to take it as such. Rotting is part of the decomposition process, and there is some hope that perhaps this is the beginning of the end for the blood.

Still, people are advised to be cautious when outside, because the smell could be overwhelming for some.

11.

I shouldn't have read so much about the bones right before bed. I'm caught now in the unsettled rest of semiconscious nightmares. Of skeletons with hair, their fleshless fingers clacking against my window, their jaws hooked open in sinister impressions of smiles.

They want me.

I don't know where this thought comes from, but I just have the strongest feeling that it's true, that the skeletons want me to come out there where they can drag me down into their gory prison.

More worrying still, I find myself wanting to.

Wanting to go outside, that is. I could just sit on the front steps, couldn't I?

No. No, that's a terrible idea. It's dark and disgusting and has that horrible smell.

I press the heels of my hands into my eyes. What I really need is sleep, but that's clearly going to elude me, at least for now.

Human blood, human bones, human hair.

This is all about us, but knowing that doesn't help. We've done a lot of bad stuff as a species. I could go through one day's worth of world news and have a pages-long list of human atrocities. And that's ignoring the damages we've done to the planet itself, the irreversible ones, the ones we like to pretend aren't real. This disaster could be a response to any one of those things. Or it could be an accumulation; we've used up all the earth's patience over the millennia, and now it's just done with us. Or it could be God. Skimming the Bible a little more, I discovered that despite what he said to Noah, he still found plenty of ways to punish people. So as hard as it is for me to believe a creator could be so cruel, the possibility's always there.

Or it could have nothing to do with us at all. Maybe it was destined to happen no matter what. We assume it's never happened before because why would it have, but screw asteroids and tar pits and climate change; maybe something like this is what actually killed off the dinosaurs way back when.

I pick up my phone to check the time. Ten fifteen. It's not even late. That might be my problem—I tried to go to bed too early.

The phone buzzes, startling me so bad I almost drop it onto my face. Aracely is calling me.

"I'm so bored," she says when I answer.

"Me, too. I tried to sleep, but I don't think I'm tired enough."

"I'm really . . . sick of this," she says.

"Me, too."

"I'm home alone. It's a little creepy."

"Where's your dad?"

"Got called to tow someone. And, whatever, he does that all the time. But when I was with Marina earlier, she told me some guy showed up at the police station last night with a knife, shouting about doom and stuff, and tried to stab one of the officers."

"Jesus."

"I know." She sighs. I hear it as a puff of static through my phone. "So I just keep thinking about it, and that's why I'm . . . Dammit, I swear I didn't call you just to whine. But apparently that's what I'm doing."

"It's okay! I'd be freaked out, too. Besides, even if you *did* call just to vent, I wouldn't mind."

"You wouldn't?"

"Of course not."

"Good to know." Her voice holds a smile. "Hey, I'm sorry I didn't go with you at school. I was happy to walk with Marina, and we ended up meeting some other friends, but I felt like . . . I don't know. Like I should have been braver."

"Actually, *I* meant to apologize for not walking with you."

"Clearly, one of us is being too polite," she says.

"Pretty sure it's you."

"Maybe it's both of us."

"See? It's totally you. You did it again, just now."

"You're right, I *was* being polite just now, because clearly it's you."

We both laugh.

"So what're your plans now that we're free from school but trapped at home?" she asks.

"Basically, my plan is to figure out how to get untrapped. And otherwise . . . be bored. You?"

"I don't know." She sighs again. "Maybe I'll try to get to the library. I feel like I've already done everything there is to do at home, other than read. What do people *do* who don't go outdoors?"

"No idea. First thing I'm doing when this is over is going on a nice, long hike."

"Me, too. We can go together."

"Sounds good to me."

"I just hope it's soon," she says. "I spent, like, three hours looking at shoes earlier. Did you know they make high-heeled rain boots? But of course I can't order them because the company's not shipping anything right now."

"Oh my God, would you ever get along well with my friend Cadence," I tell her.

"I hope I get to meet her before too long. I . . ."

There's a sound on her end, and then a muffled male voice says something I can't make out.

"I'm on the phone," Aracely replies to the voice.

"Well, say good night, Aracely. Time to go to bed." *That* I hear.

She heaves an impressive sigh, then says to me, "Sorry, I have to go. Dad's home. Talk to you tomorrow?"

"Yeah, sounds good."

I should talk to Aracely *every* night before bed, I think. Just the sound of her voice makes me happier.

Things may not be good right now, but I'm fortunate that I'm not going through this alone. I get to suffer this out in a comfortable house, knowing that I'm surrounded by people who care what happens to me. I shouldn't forget that, ever, because to be cared about is no insignificant thing.

In the morning, I find myself sitting on the front stoop, just like I convinced myself not to yesterday. I'm pretending to be observing the blood while actually watching my neighbors across the street have a pretty epic screaming match in their front yard about who gets to use the car.

It's interesting to watch people interact this way; there's so much passion behind it, but such a negative kind of passion.

I think screaming like that would really make my throat hurt.

The argument concludes with the woman slamming shut the car door and the man slamming the house door, and now my street is dead quiet. I don't like the quiet; it's unnaturally thick, much like the fetid air I can barely stand to breathe.

But Mom left me a long list of chores, and if I go inside, I'll feel obligated to do them.

That's how I'm explaining it to myself, anyway. My reasoning for being out here. Because the idea that something *compelled* me out here . . . My brain shuts down when I try to process any such notion.

A door opens a couple houses over, and I watch a man who's about my dad's age emerge. He lights up a cigarette and leans against the rail surrounding his porch. He looks . . . peaceful. But how could he be? How is he not rushing through his cigarette and flying back indoors?

Do I look peaceful, too?

Our eyes meet, and for a second, the man looks ashamed. But then he takes an extra long drag off his cigarette, and it's like a nicotine addict's version of a shrug.

I should get up. Go back indoors. But I don't *want* to, and that's scary as fuck.

It's so terrible out here, so hard to breathe, so disgusting and vile. And yet, out here, I feel comforted. Like this is how things are meant to be, and everything will be all right.

My phone beeps with a text that I hope is from Hillary, because we were going to figure out how to make this no-school thing less miserable.

It's not from Hillary. It's from the mobile alert system. I open it, curious.

ALERT. Do not drink or touch liquids possibly contaminated by blood. For more information, visit cdc.gov.

What the hell? I recoil from the pond that is my yard, edging back indoors.

I pry off my boots with extra caution, sidestepping the smears of blood around our entryway, and head straight for the laptop in my room.

I don't even have to go to the CDC's site to get more information. CNN—which I've had as my homepage since all this started—blazes with the bold, all-caps headline: BREAKING NEWS: TOXINS FOUND IN BLOOD.

I scan it with a tightening knot in my stomach. So there it goes. Our water supply. Not all of it, but most of it. We can't drink anything that might've been contaminated, have to keep any such substances away from our noses and mouths, because accidental ingestion of the blood itself would be even worse.

There's a toxin in it, they discovered, that causes "severe psychological distress." And if you're showing any symptoms of such distress, you're to go to a hospital right away because you can become an extreme danger to yourself or others. This is not to be taken lightly, the article says; this can be deadly. Anxiously, I read the list of symptoms:

- Vivid, unusual nightmares
- Losing track of what happened during periods of time
- Memory loss
- Hallucinations
- Delusions
- Paranoia
- Unusual thoughts or behaviors, even if not listed

Mostly nothing on that list applies to me, but nightmares . . .

I assumed the nightmares I've been having were a sign of a different sort of psychological distress. The expected kind; the kind that goes away. We learned about it in psych class: most people have stress reactions to trauma, and I figured I'm traumatized enough that nightmares are no surprise. But was I wrong? Are they a sign of something worse, something dangerous?

My phone rings as I'm searching for more information. It's Dad, so I answer.

"Have you seen the news?" he asks.

"Yeah."

"Okay. So you'll be very careful and only drink bottled water?"

"Yes, Dad."

"Good. I'll be home on time tonight, so I'll see you and Mom in a while, okay?"

"All right, I'll tell her."

I hang up, trying not to be annoyed, because if I *hadn't* seen the news, I would've appreciated his call. I spend the next hour or so reading more about the toxin, how it's unfamiliar and was hidden within the structure of the blood, which is why it took so long to discover.

It's not deadly, so there's that, but apparently the "psychological distress" has caused people to do some pretty crazy things, which isn't really better. Especially since they don't know yet how—or if—you can be helped. I should've probably seen this coming. There was that girl Cadence mentioned, from her sister's college. And the man Aracely told me about last night. People who were fine before and then suddenly just *lost* it.

Thinking about it makes me feel shuddery and ill.

What if I'm having delusions and I don't even know? How *do* you know if you're having delusions? Could my compulsion earlier to go outdoors be a sign of something? Wait— is my fear about it now paranoia? I start to search for more information, but hear the front door open.

"Lea?" Mom calls.

Crap. I haven't done *any* of the chores she left me.

I scurry out to greet her, hoping she'll forgive me, since it's only ten in the morning and she shouldn't be home from work at the collectibles distributor till four.

"Hey, Mom, I—" I stop dead. Mom stands in the doorway with a giant container of water in each hand, and a spectacularly gruesome black eye. "Are you okay?" I rush to take one of the water containers from her. "What happened?"

"Oh, don't worry, I'm fine." She steps out of her boots. "I left work early and stopped at the grocery store. Things were a little . . . volatile there."

"A *little*? Your eye, it's . . . You should put something on that, Mom. An ice pack."

Up close, it looks even worse. Frostbite black, swollen, shiny.

"Really, Lea, I'm fine. We needed water. And now we have it. Help me clean up our supply?"

I sense this is non-optional, so I follow her into the hall where she separates the safe-to-drink water we got from bottled sources or from that first night, when our tap water was blood-free.

All the rest, we dump down the drain. Bucket after bucket. It's hard to watch it go, but a relief to see how much still remains afterward. More than I expected.

Dad made sure we were well-prepared right from the beginning, and I'm grateful.

"So, Mom," I say, dabbing nervously at a wet spot on the counter. "I read earlier that if you have symptoms of, like, psychological problems, you should go to the hospital . . ."

"You think *I'm* having symptoms?" she asks, eyebrows knitted. Her eyes flit to the Bible sitting on the end table.

"Uh, no. I meant . . . Well, they listed nightmares. And I've been . . . I've had them lots lately."

"Oh, I don't think they mean nightmares like you've had. You don't need to worry, sweetheart."

I don't know what to say. I want her to dismiss it more confidently—without using qualifiers like *I don't think*—and I want her to back up her dismissal with something solid. Because, if they don't mean nightmares about blood and skeletons and hair that strangles, what kind of nightmares *do* they mean?

"I just worry that since we don't really know what they mean by any of it—"

"Lea, listen to me." Mom takes me by the shoulders and stares uncomfortably into my eyes. Her fingers dig, claw-like, into my flesh. "You are not sick. You're an imaginative girl, and this is a scary experience for all of us. I promise, if I thought something was wrong, I'd get you to the doctor right away. Haven't I always?"

"Yes," I mumble.

"All right, then." She straightens and smiles. "Why don't you go relax for a while? You can do the rest of your chores later."

"Sure."

Mom leaves me to myself with the idea that she's helped. She hums happily in her own bedroom and I try to feel that way, too: happy, or at least calm.

But I don't.

I can try to convince myself I'm fine all I want, but I've seen it now, that list of symptoms. It's in my mind, freaking me out, and I can't begin to figure out how to make it leave.

12.

I've decided it's time Aracely and Hillary spend some real time together. That's a lie. *Hillary* decided it, yesterday.

"I barely know her!" she said. "And I'm, like, the only person besides your parents who knows you're dating. It might be fun for her. Maybe she'll decide she wants more people to know."

"I'll see if she's up for it. Probably she will be." I didn't mention that I doubted it'd impact much—Aracely will be ready to come out when she's ready.

Hillary understands the emotions of coming out about as well as a straight person can, but she's never had to do it, so she can only fathom it from an external perspective. The biggest flaw in her perspective is that she believes everyone will handle it the same way she did. She can't grasp the idea that Aracely's friends might have a harder time being supportive than mine. That maybe Aracely has had feelings for one of them in the past and it makes them uncomfortable, or that they might be offended if she hasn't. Aracely's friends seem great. She says nothing but good things about them, but I understand, more than Hillary ever could, why Aracely hasn't come out to them yet. You don't want it to be this thing you have to say. You just want to feel how you feel, and not have it matter. But it does. And it might change nothing. Her relationships with her friends might go on just as ever.

But it also might change everything. If Aracely isn't prepared yet to potentially face that, then I will keep on being patient. And even though I wish we could openly be a couple, I am truly okay with waiting until she's ready.

Despite all that, Aracely did agree—nervously—to hang out with Hillary this morning. They've only met a couple times, briefly. Being a year apart in school, they don't have a ton of opportunities to run into each other. So this'll be good, I think. They'll like each other. Of course, I've been up since five, fidgety with irrational worry that they won't.

Both my parents and Hillary's are at work this morning, and Hillary's little brother is at her aunt's, so Hillary is coming to pick up Aracely and me from my house at nine thirty, even though her parents firmly forbade her from driving anywhere.

My doorbell rings. I glance at the clock. Eight forty-five. Right on time.

Aracely smiles when I open the door to let her in. An extra forty-five minutes alone with Aracely wasn't part of Hillary's plan. But it really enhances the plan, in my opinion.

Aracely's just wearing jeans and a T-shirt, but she looks beautiful; she always does. While she removes her boots, I scan the house, one last time, for anything out of place. Nothing is, of course. I made sure of it earlier. I even arranged the magazines on the coffee table in the most perfectly disheveled way I could manage. Our house looks as normal as a house can look. Except—

"Whoa," Aracely says, her eyes fixed on the dining table. On the cups, bowls, pans filled with water.

Yeah, nothing I could do about *that*. If only the dining room and living room had separating walls. I could have closed the door and she would never have seen.

"Tip of the iceberg," I say, tilting my head toward the hallway, lined with buckets and heavy store-bought containers of water.

"We should have done this, too, probably." Her eyes drift from the buckets to the wide arch leading into the kitchen. Where we've got more water—bottled—plus piles and piles of canned goods and other nonperishables. "We had an okay supply of Brita filters and stuff, but after yesterday's news . . . We've got *some* water still but nowhere near this amount."

"I'm sure this'll get figured out before we need much of it, so . . ." I shrug. I shouldn't be embarrassed; it isn't like we live this way always. But it's the first time Aracely has visited my house. I wish it was less weird.

She looks like she might say something more about the water, but changes her mind. "So what should I know about Hillary? What should I say to her? To like . . . impress her."

She bites a nail, looking up at me from under her lashes in an anxious sort of way.

"You'll be fine. I swear you will. She just cares that you're a nice person. She's not looking for reasons to hate you or anything. She knows that I—" Heat flares in my cheeks. I can never tell if I'm visibly blushing or not. Based on the smile creeping slowly onto her face, I'm guessing I am.

"That you *what*?" she presses, leaning closer to me.

The scent of her perfume wafts deliciously toward me, stronger than normal. Covering the smell of not bathing, I'm guessing. I did the same thing.

"That I like you," I say with forced nonchalance.

"I already know you like me." Her smile is wider. "Otherwise, I'd hope you wouldn't be dating me."

"A lot, then. I like you a lot."

"Well, I like you a lot, too. So."

I smile back at her, but I'm not quite sure what to do with myself now. Do I kiss her? Say something else? Stand here, fiddling with my lip ring, and stare at her like an idiot? That last one can't possibly be the best choice, yet that's exactly what I'm doing. I clear my throat, and use it as an excuse to break eye contact. I am so smooth.

"There is no way to say this right now without sounding like I have ulterior motives, but maybe instead of standing in the doorway, we should go in my room."

She laughs. "Is there *ever* a way to say that without sounding like you have ulterior motives?"

"Probably not."

We squeeze down the hall, which was kind of narrow to begin with and now is barely a foot wide thanks to the buckets.

"I'm so jealous of how big your room is." Aracely makes herself at home immediately, sitting atop my bed and smoothing my quilt with her fingers.

"I'm jealous of your river view."

"My river view would be way better if I were nearer the covered bridge. Unless I look, like, straight down, it's pretty much just a view of that dumb bike shop."

"Still." I sit beside her, our arms brushing. My skin sparks with delighted shivers.

Maybe I didn't have ulterior motives in the exact moment when I invited her into my room, but I *did* have ulterior motives when I invited her to come over forty-five minutes before Hillary's arrival. Okay, fine. My motives were never pure. My stomach flutters when she turns her head toward me and our eyes meet. We just both said that we like each other *a lot*, and I feel like that's got to mean something. It might not be love—yet—but it is significant.

I brush my lips over hers, a feather of a touch. Then again, just as lightly. She catches my chin between her fingertips.

"No ulterior motives, huh?" she says, arching an eyebrow.

"Don't pretend you didn't know that was a total lie."

She laughs, and it's like sunlight, filling my room with warmth and light and joy. We kiss again, and it's now that I feel the change our confessions from a few minutes ago have brought. I feel it in the intensity of her kiss, the certainty of her hands around my waist. We are not casual anymore. We are something. And I could not be happier about it.

"Hello!" I hear Hillary call from the front door.

"Be right there!" I shout back, disentangling myself hurriedly from Aracely.

I completely lost track of time and now, shit, I really hope Hillary does not come in my room, because I don't need that kind of awkward. Aracely smooths her curls and straightens her clothes while I try to figure out how to rehook my bra. It's all I can do not to burst into laughter as we emerge straight-faced and casual from my room, like Hillary doesn't know exactly what we were doing in there.

She's standing in the entry, boots still on, a smirk on her face. "So *that's* why you said you thought eight thirty was too early," she teases. "I should've known it wasn't because you'd still be sleeping, you liar."

I smack her on the arm. "Shut up."

Her smirk changes into a more genuine smile when she turns her attention to Aracely. "I'm glad we're finally going to get to spend some time together. Lea's said a lot about you."

Aracely smiles shyly back at her. "She's said a lot about you, too."

"Good things, I hope."

"Nah." I look up from pulling on my rain boots. "I only ever tell people horrible things about you."

"You are in rare form today," Hillary says, opening the door for Aracely and me to leave the house before her. She pulls a scarf up over her mouth, and Aracely and I follow suit.

Despite the scarf, the horrible smell of the outdoors hits me like a punch to the throat. I'd forgotten. My house isn't completely free of the stench, but it's not so eye-wateringly awful indoors. It's more vaguely unpleasant, like if a mouse died in the walls. And yet, despite the overwhelming stink, there's a part of me that wants to be out here, that revels in it somehow. A *delusional* part; it has to be. I swallow and shake that thought off. I'm not delusional; I'm *not*. I just like the outdoors, and blood or not, it feels good to be away from my house.

Yeah. That's what it is.

We slosh extra carefully through the blood, mindful now that the consequences of falling into and ingesting blood would be much worse than feeling disgusted. I run my fingers over my arms.

None of the news reports were very clear about whether it's a problem if the blood gets somewhere else, too, like cuts or scrapes. The implication seemed to be that it's not a concern, but my trust in those sorts of analyses is gone now.

I checked myself thoroughly last night for even the tiniest of scratches and found nothing, but I still don't quite feel comfortable.

Aracely and I both slide into the backseat of Hillary's car. My hand finds its way into Aracely's, and she smiles at me—I can tell by the crinkles at the corners of her eyes.

Hillary glances at us through the rearview mirror. "Hang on back there. Driving was wicked rough on the way over. Main Street's closed for cleanup right now, so I had to go the long way."

Diligently, we both strap on our seat belts.

Hillary was not lying about the drive. Her car slams over bones like one of those horrible fair rides you fear will fly apart at any second. She's only going ten miles an hour, but it feels too fast. And even with the windows rolled up and the AC and heat off, the blood's ever-worsening stench seeps into the vehicle. It's all I can do not to gag.

Maybe we shouldn't have come out at all. The news was very clear that the toxins aren't airborne, but could they be wrong about that, too? I've never been anywhere in my life where the stench of the air so deeply pervaded my senses. And I've been in a chicken barn in the summer, so that's saying something.

We make it around a harrowing curve where once there were railroad tracks, but not long after that Hillary's car starts making a really worrying noise. A high-pitched whine-hum.

"Uh, Hillary?" I say hesitantly.

"I know." She slows even further. "But what can I do? We've got to make it to my house and then . . . I don't know.

We'll figure it out."

The car coughs and lurches. Hillary pulls it over into the dirt parking lot of a truck terminal. Mostly, anyway, because the car stalls before she's completely off the road.

She twists the key. The radio and lights come back to life, but it's like the battery has died.

"You have enough gas, right?" I ask. Fear sits like sickness in my gut.

She throws me a death glare via the rearview. "I don't know what's wrong. Everything was fine earlier."

She opens the door, then slams it shut, cursing voraciously, when blood rushes into the car. I press my face to the window. It's high right here—the blood. Like it probably would be on Main Street, except Main Street has better drainage, which keeps it under control. A trickle of red sneaks under the edge of my door, and I flinch back.

"Shit, Hillary, it's getting in your car!"

"I *know*!" she shouts back at me.

I resist the urge to pull up my feet. My boots will protect me. I checked them this morning for holes. They're definitely fine.

"What do we do now?" Aracely's voice holds an edge of panic. She sits stiffly on her side of the car, eyeing the road and Hillary and me in turn.

"Triple A?" I suggest. "We've got to get out of here."

Hillary tries turning the key again. The car gurgles, like it's drowning. "Shit," she mutters. "My parents are going to fucking kill me. I should've listened. *Fuck*, this was a bad idea."

She calls AAA but gets no one. It's just a recorded

message about being out of service on account of the "disaster." The blood isn't trickling in very quickly, but the car's floor is spongy with liquid.

"I'll call my dad," Aracely says. "He'll come get us. Just if he asks, you guys know my friend Jenna, and she had you pick me up to go to her house. Okay?"

Hillary meets my eye in the rearview. I quickly look down at my lap.

"We can do that," I say.

"Thanks, Aracely," Hillary adds.

"No problem." Aracely dials her father. Her voice is calm as she explains the situation, and I can't really hear his end of the conversation, which means he must not be yelling, at least, but the set of her jaw and her periodic cringes suggest that he's angry with her. Maybe she wasn't supposed to come out, either. I never asked.

"He's on his way," Aracely says tightly after she hangs up.

I slip my hand around hers. The tension in her body diminishes, but only slightly.

The three of us wait in an uncomfortable silence. Hillary keeps trying to start her car, and it keeps gurgling and refusing.

"I don't *think* the blood is higher than boot level out there. I could go look under the hood," Aracely offers hesitantly. "My dad's a mechanic. I know a little."

"Okay." Hillary pops the hood. "Just be careful. *Seriously* careful. I don't like this."

Aracely opens her door very cautiously. The blood barely reaches the bottom of the door, but a little sloshes in and I cringe. What a mess.

"We should look, too," I tell Hillary, readjusting the scarf over my mouth.

"Yeah." She doesn't want to, I can tell, but she knows I'm right. Leaving Aracely alone outside is a bad idea. Just in case.

We join Aracely at the front of the car. We have to move in a shuffly way so as not to make waves in the blood, because it's *really* close to the tops of our boots. I kick several bones and snag my toe on hair a couple times.

"I think there's blood in the engine," Aracely informs us. "I don't know how, but . . . I'm pretty sure. It's flooded. Dad'll have to tow you."

"Dammit." Hillary frowns down at all the metal and plastic beneath her hood. "I had no idea that was possible."

"Me neither," Aracely says. "I don't think it's—"

I scream. Something has me by the ankle. It tugs—tugs hard, tightening, cutting off circulation. It's the fucking hair, I just know it.

"Something's grabbing me!" I yell, because Aracely and Hillary are staring at me like I've lost it.

Aracely wraps her arms around my waist and pulls. I push with my free foot, but my other is stuck fast.

The hair around it jerks, and Aracely almost loses her grip on me, but Hillary gets hold of my leg and helps pull.

Slowly, slowly, I come free, but my boot stays rooted.

"Close the hood!" Aracely orders Hillary. Then practically throws me onto it. I scrabble back nearly to the windshield, shaking. Hillary joins me, folding an arm around my shoulders.

But Aracely, she goes after my boot.

"Just leave it!" I say tearfully.

"*No*." She is emphatic.

She leverages herself against the car's front bumper and pulls with all her strength. Finally, there's a tearing sound and my boot wrenches free. Aracely falls back onto the hood, breathing hard, holding up my boot like the hard-won prize it is.

She gives it back to me, and I grudgingly pull it on. Hair still encircles it, a thick layer, like an entire ponytail wrapped itself around my foot. Aracely plucks at it in a compulsive sort of way, tearing it free strand by bloody strand. Her eyes are bright, like she's blinking back tears.

"Are you okay, Lea?" Hillary asks, squeezing my shoulder.

I nod. I'm still processing what just happened. Because God, I don't *want* to process it. Aracely looks pale—at least, in comparison to usual—and I think this affected her as much as it did me. I close my fingers around her forearm, tugging her hand gently away from my boot. "I'm fine. I'll cut it with scissors at home. And . . . thank you."

She smiles tremblingly at me. "You're welcome."

And then she clambers the rest of the way up the hood to sit on my other side, pressing her face into my neck for just a moment. Her shaky exhale caresses my skin but does nothing to slow my pulse.

"Well, this day is not going quite like I thought it would," Hillary says. She peers around me to look at Aracely. "I'm so sorry. I'm such a moron."

"It isn't your fault." Aracely shifts a little so she's more visually accessible to Hillary. "How could you have known the blood would . . . you know, would do . . . that?"

A truck drives up to us, a big pickup with much more clearance than Hillary's little sedan. I recognize Aracely's father from pictures at their house.

"Here goes," Aracely says breezily.

Her father gets out of the truck. He appears well-prepared for this, wearing waders, the kind meant for serious fishermen, like waterproof overalls. And he has a hunting knife strapped to his belt.

"Car trouble?" he asks with a forced grin. His tone belies his attempt at lightening the situation.

"The engine's flooded," Aracely says. "But, um, with blood."

Her dad nods. "I figured. Saw it a couple times at work earlier in the week. Which of you owns this car?"

"That's me," Hillary says. "I'm Hillary. I really, really appreciate this."

"What were you girls thinking, driving around in this?"

He's still looking at Hillary when he asks, but I have a feeling this question is for Aracely.

"We weren't thinking," Aracely says. "I should have told you I was leaving the house. I'm sorry."

"Well." He frowns. "I think it's fair to say you learned a lesson?"

"Yes." Her voice is barely a whisper.

"Okay. Go wait in the truck. I'm gonna figure out how to hook this on, and then I'll get you kids home."

I don't want to step back down into the blood, but it is a small comfort to know that there's someone nearby who could easily cut me free.

The three of us jump into the back of the truck's extended

cab. I'm in the middle again, and now, in the safety of the truck, every tiny brush of Aracely's arm against mine feels magnified by a thousand.

"I didn't know the blood and stuff could attack people," Hillary says quietly.

"I guess it makes sense," I say. "I mean, just by *existing*, it's attacking us. So this shouldn't be all that unexpected."

"And yet everything it does still manages to surprise us all," Aracely says in a tired voice.

And she's right. The blood is continually taking the world by surprise, even though by now it would be logical if we all assumed the worst. We haven't, though, and I don't know if we will.

It's just, it's still so hard to accept that this is real.

FAQ: Government-provided respirators

Why do I want a respirator? Respirators will help you breathe more easily in less-than-ideal air quality conditions. They are particularly recommended for those who may already have breathing difficulties, such as those suffering from asthma.

What happens if I can't get one? You may find yourself having a little more difficulty breathing outdoors without one, however, you **should not panic**. The air is not toxic, and you will continue to be safe, despite the discomfort.

Where do I get a respirator? Click <u>here</u> for a list of respirator distribution sites by zip code.

How much does it cost? For the time being, respirators are being given out at no cost to citizens.

What if I already own a respirator? You are encouraged to use your own respirator, if you have one. This will allow more people to benefit from the limited supplies of government-provided respirators. **Do not** try to sell personal respirators.

What else do I need to know? Supplies are finite. If you want to ensure that you get one, we recommend that you get to your distribution site early. Limit one respirator per person. Parents may ask for additional respirators for children under the age of 14. You will be fitted upon arrival at the distribution site, so anyone who will be receiving a mask must be present.

Until further notice, private sale of respirators is prohibited.
If you are found selling a respirator, you will be prosecuted.

13.

I swallow nausea as I stand outside the courthouse in blood that's only a couple of inches below the tops of my boots. It rose again during the night. Not by a lot, but if it keeps rising a little bit at a time, eventually . . . well, I don't want to think about eventually.

I came here by shuttle, which is a thing we have now, and although it wasn't a long trip, it also wasn't pleasant.

The post office/courthouse building is where they've had a food-and-water bank set up for a while, but now it's also our local respirator distribution center.

Last night, regional news announced shuttles would start running this morning so no one has to walk in unsafe conditions to get here. One of the stops is two houses over from mine, so I managed to flee while Mom was in her room reading her Bible. Her work finally decided yesterday to shut down for the foreseeable future—no one's buying frivolous collectibles right now; they can't afford to pay employees to do nothing. After what happened the other day with Hillary's car, Mom's put me on a lockdown of sorts. I can't blame her, especially since I didn't even tell her about the hair—the worst, most terrifying part of what happened. But I decided it was worth the risk to sneak out today. Mom said we don't need respirators if we aren't leaving the house— and Dad, who still has to go to work, has owned a respirator for ages—but I want to be prepared, just in case.

So here I am with a Swiss army knife tucked in my jeans pocket, since the last thing I want is to be caught with hair wrapped around my boot and no way to free myself. I feel pretty good about my decision. Despite the thickness in the air and the weight of anxiety in my gut, it feels great to be out.

"Just you?" asks the woman behind the counter when I reach the front of the line.

"Yes, thank you." I'd get one for Mom, but it's not allowed.

The woman measures my face in a bunch of different ways, then makes some adjustments to a respirator and hands it to me with a brochure about its proper use. I hesitate. Holding this creepy mask in my hands makes me so uncomfortable, I almost want to give it back. I mean, what do I do with this? I want to ask the woman, who smiles understandingly at me, but the man who's next in line is pressing his beer gut against my back.

Near the door, I put on my respirator using the diagram in my brochure as a guide. There's a pause between the moment when I start to inhale and when air rushes into my lungs. It's like watching a TV show where the sound and picture aren't quite lined up. You want to get used to it, but you can't. The mask makes my face feel moist, and I don't like the way it presses on the bridge of my nose. But it's better than breathing toxic filth, that's for sure.

I reach into my pocket, closing my fingers around my Swiss army knife. It may be tiny, but its presence is a comfort. The idea of the hair ensnaring me again makes me shudder. A small knife is probably better, anyway. Less chance I'll accidentally saw into my leg during a panicked moment.

Part of me wishes I could stay here in this post office/courthouse building forever. Something about its efficient, high-ceilinged design makes me feel safe. It is a building that knows its own importance and is not afraid to show it off.

But I can't stay here, because that would be stupid. And because the sooner I get home, the less mad Mom will be. She knows I'm here. I couldn't exactly ignore when she texted me (though I *did* ignore when she called). She's definitely angry, but if I return promptly, I hope she won't be *too* angry. So I push open the door and step out into the sunlight. Immediately, I spot Aracely coming up the wide stairs. She looks up, our eyes meet, and her face splits into a grin.

"Sexy!" she teases, stopping in front of me and poking my respirator in the nose.

"You'll look just as good in yours, I'm sure," I say. My voice is strange, forcing its way through the microphone built into the mask.

"Not possible. Come on. Wait with me while I get mine. Please?"

I shrug. I should go home. I can practically feel Mom glaring at me through the phone that sits in my pocket. But I'm in a safe place and I want to see Aracely, so . . . Mom can just deal. What's she going to do, anyway? I'm already not allowed out.

Part of me feels guilty, suddenly, for not having texted any of my friends to meet me here. But, then, I didn't text Aracely, either. It was just a coincidence. An excellent one.

Still, once we're back in line, I send Hillary a quick message, just so she knows I haven't forgotten her existence.

She replies almost immediately with, *Don't worry about it! Levi's over. We totally forgot about resps. Will prob get them later, mom wants me to for finn. Doing other stuff right now instead if you know what I mean ;)*

Ew. No, *not* ew. I'm supposed to be getting along with Levi. But still, the image of them doing *other stuff* grosses me out.

"Excuse me." A woman behind us prods my shoulder with an overlong fake fingernail. "You can't be in line if you already have a respirator. You only get one."

"I'm not trying to get another one," I snap. "I'm just waiting in line with my friend."

"I'll be watching, you know. I'll see if you take another one."

I glare at her in the nastiest way I know how. "You do that."

"Asshole," Aracely mutters under her breath.

The woman doesn't hear, but I do, and my snort of laughter in response earns me another poke from the talon. "Is something funny?" she asks aggressively.

"Nothing to do with you," I lie, though I'm suppressing laughter again and I'm pretty sure the look on my face makes that clear. Really, though. It isn't like I've got the respirator stuffed down my pants. I'm holding it right in my hands. I'm obviously not trying anything.

The woman huffs, but I ignore her, paying attention instead to how Aracely keeps shifting closer to me, so that our hands are sort of brushing. It's the closest thing to PDA I'm probably going to get, at least for now, and it sends all kinds of sparks down into my belly.

"Your dad been busy?" I ask, because if I don't do something other than fixate my whole attention on our brushing knuckles, I am going to ignite.

"Incredibly. He's gone, like, all the time now."

"Hmm." Gone all the time. That sure gets the wheels turning in my head.

She fixes me with a flirty-shy half-smirk. "He pays our neighbor to keep an eye on me."

"Hmm." Damn.

"But she can't tell any of my friends apart."

"Hmm."

She grins wider. "Is that all you know how to say?"

"Apparently."

Her phone dings, and I'm disappointed when she uses the hand that was touching mine to pull it from her pocket. "Sorry," she says when she puts it away. "My friend Brian. He wanted to know how the blood is down this way. He's not sure if he wants to come."

"I don't blame him." The blood *does* seem to be a bit deeper here than higher up on the hills, though it works around the laws of gravity to an extent, just like it works around all the other laws of nature. "But I think it's worth the risk."

Finally, we've made it to the front of the line. I can feel the talon-clawed lady staring lasers into the back of my head, and I *so badly* want to ask for another respirator just to spite her. But they wouldn't give me one anyway, and I don't want to start some kind of hostile mob situation, so I don't.

"How do I look?" Aracely asks in her garbled mask voice once she's figured out how to put it on.

"I think we'll start a new fashion trend," I answer.

She flips her hair in an imitation of a sultry supermodel, and we both laugh as we walk down the steps outside.

There's no room for laughter on the street, though. The shuttle's just pulling away as we approach, so either we walk or we wait here for who knows how long until the next one arrives.

We pick walking. Very, very carefully.

The web of hair hidden beneath the blood's surface is wicked thick at this point. It bothers me more than anything else. Because it's *hair*. Other people's hair. Dead people's hair. And not just from their heads. Every step is gooey, like a wet carpet, and the memory of strands twining around my ankle is still all too fresh.

We keep our arms linked. The town has done its best to keep bones off streets and sidewalks; I've seen piles of them, stark white with hair twisted around them like thread on a spool. But even still, the blood hides all manner of obstacles—missed bones, broken sidewalk, extra thick tangles of hair—and people still help each other through it whenever possible. Which makes this okay. Makes it explainable, if someone saw us.

Suddenly, there's a loud *crack* and Aracely goes down, splashing into the blood, barely managing to keep her face out of it. A man stands over her with a big leg bone, and now he's trying to yank the respirator off her face.

"Get away from her!" I scream.

"They ran out of respirators," he snarls, eyeing mine now, too.

"So *what*?" I shout back. "It's not like you'll die without one."

"If you want to believe that, good for you."

His attention turns back to Aracely, struggling to pull herself up out of the blood. Her arms are snared with long strands of hair.

Fury seizes my heart. This is not how people are supposed to behave.

I yank on the bone, catching the man off guard, and rip it from his grasp. I pound him in the ribs with it until he backs off, swearing at me and shielding himself with his arms.

"Come on!" I shout, tossing the bone into a bush and holding out a hand to Aracely.

She takes it, and I flinch at the thick warmth of the blood that covers her skin. We run, stumbling over things, but mercifully staying on our feet until we reach her building, where we both collapse at the base of the indoor stairwell.

Aracely's breathing is loud and whimpery, and I realize she's crying.

"You didn't get any in your mouth or anything, right?"

She shakes her head but cries even harder.

"It's okay." I reach for her, ignoring the fact that we are both now spattered with blood and clumps of hair. "It's okay. We're safe."

"We're *not* safe," she sobs into my shoulder. "We'll never be safe again."

She's right. I know she is. Respirators and attacks in the street and reports that water supplies are running low. Blood that rises steadily, hair that wraps around limbs, bones that pop tires and trip feet. Toxins we can't ingest without losing our minds. I've viciously harmed someone, which makes me feel all wrong inside, even if he deserved it.

This is the beginning of the end.

14.

I'm grounded. *Super* grounded.

When I got home from Aracely's in my blood-spattered clothes, I obviously couldn't hide from my mother that something had gone wrong. I downplayed it as much as I could when I explained, but she still flipped out.

Now I'm lying on my bed, holding the respirator in my hands, trying not to think about this morning.

The smell is bothering me again; I wish I could move my bed away from the window. It feels like I'm inhaling toxins, even though I know I'm not. But how can air smell so bad and not be poisonous? I close my eyes. It's not even that fucking strong in here. It's got to be in my head. Like a hallucination. Or would it be a delusion? No. Neither. My head is *fine*.

With a growl in my throat, I jump up and start pacing. *Knowing* I'm not allowed out makes it so much worse. I know I can't leave, but I want to do *something*.

THIS SUCKS, I text Hillary.

Come over, she responds.

Can't. Mom's got me locked down.

Want me to come there?

Idk. Let me check if u can.

I find Mom in the living room. She's eyeing her Bible again. It unsettles me a little bit when she does that. The thing has disappeared and reappeared more times over the past days. It's like she wants to find answers within it, but she's still so messed up from her uber-religious childhood, she hasn't quite gotten the courage.

"Can Hillary come over?" I ask.

Mom is silent for long enough that I know she's trying to think of a reason to say no. "I guess I can't see why not," she says finally. "If her mother allows."

Mom clearly thought requiring permission from Hillary's mom would work in her favor, but fortunately for me, the hospital is one of a dwindling number of places in town that hasn't closed, and as both of Hillary's parents work very long hours there, she's free to decide for herself about coming over. Which means, twenty minutes later, she's at my house, Finn in tow.

Since she's been watching him while her parents work, they left her one of their SUVs, which can handle the terrain a whole lot better than her sedan. Putrid air follows her and Finn in, and their boots leave a fresh bloodstain on the carpet at the entry. I try not to look outside before she closes the door. I don't feel like seeing the mess right now.

An aboveground grave, that's what we live in.

Mom is in love with Finn and his burgeoning sense of humor and his little dimpled cheeks, so she gets out a deck of cards to play Crazy Eights with him while Hillary and I escape to my room.

"I know it's only been two days, but it feels like a *century* since I've seen you," she says, flopping onto my bed.

"I know. I'm sorry. Other than getting a respirator, I haven't been out."

"Oh! You *have* to show me it. Levi and I took Finn to get one a little while ago, but we were too late."

I remove the respirator from my desk drawer and show it to her.

"Nice." She admires it. "It was such shit! We didn't even go *that* late, but when we got to the post office, they'd closed and people were, like, rioting over it. It was pretty scary, actually. Finn cried and Levi almost got into a fistfight with some guy who tried to cut in front of us to get on the shuttle."

"Good for Levi!" For once, I'm proud of him. "Aracely and I saw some of the early rioting, I think."

I tell her what happened, and when I'm done, she looks ashen. "Holy *shit*, Lea!"

"I know." I'm shaking a little. Talking about it in full detail makes it real, and it was so fucking terrifying. The wild look in that man's eyes. I want to think that he'd already ingested blood before it happened, and he was going crazy. But he was so lucid during the whole thing. Just scared, I think, like everyone else. Just a sign of a world getting more and more desperate.

And I wasn't any better. I pummeled the shit out of him with that bone, even when he'd given up and backed off. I wanted him to hurt for attacking Aracely. I didn't know I had any such thing in me.

"Are you okay?" Hillary asks.

I nod. I'm not, actually. But I don't want to talk about it. At all. "Are you?"

She shrugs. "I'm worried about Finn. He's so young and this is so fucking scary. And I've hardly heard from anyone except you and Levi; have you? I don't know what's going on with anyone, and I miss them."

"I haven't heard much, either." I say this with some guilt, because I haven't tried too hard to reach out. I've been so wrapped up in myself and the blood and Aracely that I've not given as much thought to my friends—even Hillary—as I should. I'm breaking her rule, and I vow to text every single person who's important to me (even Mikayla) later tonight, just to see what's up with them.

Our conversation starts to fizzle. We're talked out about the blood and the danger. School isn't happening, so no gossip. We go on about Levi and Aracely for a while, but even dissecting all of our interactions with the pair of them only lasts us so long. We can't go outside. We could talk about toxins, or the worsening water shortage it has caused, but I don't even like *thinking* about that, let alone discussing it.

We settle for painting each other's nails, listening to Finn's adorable, shrieky laughter while he beats my mom at cards in the other room, and scrolling through celebrity gossip websites, even though celebrity news is pretty sparse at this point. Those kinds of websites aren't maintained too much right now. They barely even update actual news websites anymore.

"You thirsty?" I ask after a while.

"Very, actually."

I waddle out of my room, toe separators still on, and dip two cups into one of our buckets. Water glistens on the cups' exteriors, and I wonder if there will come a time when we wish we'd saved those few precious drops. I shake the cups a little. A couple droplets detach and splash back into the bucket. There.

"You guys have plenty of water at home?" I ask, sipping from my glass. I hate lukewarm water, but the fridge is stuffed with other crap. When I complained, Dad told me the temperature of my water wasn't a priority.

"Yeah, enough. Hopefully." She sips her water, too. "Dad keeps talking about making a still."

"A still? Like those things they use to make moonshine?"

She laughs. "Yeah, kind of. Except to distill water."

"So, like, to make the bloody water drinkable?" I nearly gag thinking about it. My own cup of water loses all appeal, and I taste copper at the back of my throat.

"As a last resort, I think. Because, I mean, who knows if distilling it will even make it safe, right? But if it came to it, the risk would be better than dying of dehydration."

"Girls, have you . . ." Mom stands in my doorway. She's staring at Hillary. No, at the cup in Hillary's hands.

"Have we what?" I prompt.

"Get out," she says to Hillary. "Get out now."

Hillary looks shell-shocked.

"Mom, what's going on?" I rise slowly to my feet.

"She's drinking our water. *Our water.*" Mom's voice shakes with barely controlled rage. Then, to Hillary, *"Out!"*

"I'm so sorry," Hillary whispers, and scampers out of my room without another word or glance at me.

I call after her, chase her into the hall, but she's grabbed Finn, whose laughter has turned to tears, and they're out the door without a word to me. I whirl on Mom. "What the *hell* was that? I gave her that water, you know."

"Why?" Mom shouts at me. I flinch back. I've never seen her like this.

"She was thirsty. Are you serious? It was one glass."

"Lea." Her face is ashen, but her voice is calmer now.

"There is a worldwide water shortage. The whole world. What we have now, that's all we're going to get."

She combs her fingers repeatedly through her hair. "I shouldn't have shouted at Hillary. I'm sorry. But no more friends over, all right? It's too dangerous."

"So no one can come here, and I can't go anywhere?"

She nods.

I push past her into my room and slam the door. I'm trembling so hard, I sink to the floor, because I just can't support my own weight anymore. I'm trapped. Mom is trapping me, isolating me, and *why?* The two half-drunk cups of water still sit on my desk. Are we really in such short supply that one cup will mean the difference between life and death?

My body feels numb and sick from the encounter with my mom. There's no way she's in the right. There's no way people aren't figuring out a way to get clean water for us all. Science always provides. Isn't that what Mom has told me anytime I've tried to ask her questions about religion?

I should talk to Dad about it, maybe, but he's been so exhausted with the long hours he's working, I won't want to bother him when he gets home. Mom's overreaction was extreme, but logical.

Shakily, I cross my room to my bed, where my phone sits.

I'm so sorry, I text Hillary. *Idk what the fuck happened with her. Hope u and finn are ok.*

And then I wait. And wait and wait.

She doesn't text back.

If You Must Drink Contaminated Water

Find a deep water source, if possible, and a settled one. Water will be less contaminated here.

Skim water gently off the top; try not to stir the settled blood.

Bring water to a full boil. Continue to boil for at least one minute. If you do not have the resources to further decontaminate the water, boil a little longer, and then let it cool before attempting to drink.

Distill water. There are several simple methods you can use for distillation. For more details, see back page of the brochure.

Drink slowly. If the water makes you feel ill, stop. *Do not try to suppress vomiting if ill*. Improperly decontaminated water can be dangerous to consume. Use extreme caution.

Important Note: Drinking contaminated water could seriously endanger your health and should be considered a last resort in cases of extreme dehydration.

15.

Meet us at the park at 12:30. Look apocalyptic! xo.

This text, from Cadence, feels ominous, at eleven forty-five at night.

Um, what? I text back.

Party. Post apoc theme. Everyone's gonna be there. I was supposed to tell u earlier but forgot. Meet u at the swings!

Against my better judgment, I tell her I will. It won't be the first time I've snuck out for a party, and I hope to God it won't be the last, but the blood adds an unpleasant challenge to the whole process. That, and my parents' warning about locking me in my room. But what are the odds I'll get caught this time? Pretty slim, unless something bad happens. I remember the man who attacked Aracely, but immediately shut down that line of thought. I can't be a hermit forever because of one scary thing. It's no way to live.

I text Hillary and Aracely to ask if they're going. I get a *Yes!!! :)* from Aracely and silence from Hillary, which is all she's given me since yesterday.

Knowing Aracely will be there is all it takes to override the nagging voice in my head that tries to convince me I shouldn't go. It's the logical part of me, the place in my brain that whispers *don't* when every fiber of my being wants to go outside, just to be there. When I want to swirl a fingertip in the blood, just to feel it. But this isn't about the blood, it's about my friends. It's about Aracely. I want to see them, and I think it'll be good for me, dangerous as it may be.

So. Postapocalyptic attire. I scan my closet, frowning. A postapocalyptic theme party is perfect for Cadence. She's probably been prepping all afternoon. She'll be a spectacle. I, on the other hand, don't even know where to begin. So I begin on my computer, with a quick image search for "postapocalyptic fashion." Apparently, this is quite a thing, because there are a ton of pictures, some of which are wicked cool.

My clothes still seem inadequate, but I tug on my most well-torn pair of jeans, a long, grayish tank top, and a too-short leather (okay, faux leather) jacket. With a couple of unnecessary and creatively positioned belts and a bracelet of safety pins, I figure I'll do.

When I pull on my respirator and check myself out in my full-length mirror, I have to admit: I look pretty badass. Our respirators aren't as eerie as the gas masks of yore—they're just black plastic with circular yellow filters angled off the sides, a small exhalation valve directly in front of the mouth, and a tiny microphone and speaker so that we can be heard when we talk. But still, I could land in the middle of any disaster movie and fit in quite nicely.

Although, maybe that's not a good thing.

I grab a spare pair of rubber boots out of my closet. These are just black, and they don't fit as comfortably as my other pair, which is why I haven't been wearing them. But they go better with my outfit. I check them thoroughly for holes, then recheck myself for scratches as I've been doing multiple times a day lately.

My window groans when I open it, and swampy, thick air coils indoors. I'm glad for my respirator, blocking the worst of the smell, even though I'm not sure I'll ever get used to wearing it. It's awkwardly shaped and uncomfortable, and it's hard to position it so that my lip ring isn't mashed into my teeth.

I lower myself as delicately as possible onto the ground below. Steam rises off the blood; the night air is cooler than the ground, and as much as I hate to admit it, the layer of mist filters everything through a creepy-beautiful lens.

The usual ten-minute walk from my house to the park turns into twenty because I have to pick my way across the bone-encrusted ground. I trip twice, but luckily, I regain my balance both times. Hair catches at my boots, but I pull free of that, too, without having to use my knife. This party is starting to feel like a really terrible idea. But I haven't seen my friends in days, and I miss them. I can't pass up this opportunity.

Felix and Cadence sit on the swings at the playground. I notice them long before they notice me.

As expected, Cadence is something to behold. Her bright red hair is spiked into an enormously tall fauxhawk, her eyes are rimmed heavily with artistic black makeup, and her outfit is all leather and spikes. She's even decorated her respirator so it looks less sterile and plastic, and more gas-mask-of-yore.

Felix looks relieved when he catches sight of me. He hasn't dressed up, really. His shirt has a zombie on it, but I don't think that counts.

"Where's Hill?" I ask. I can't get used to how crackly and weird my voice sounds through the mask's built-in communication device.

"She couldn't come," says Cadence.

"And hi to you, too," adds Felix.

"Sorry, hi." My face feels moist where the respirator traps the fog of my breath beneath its edges. It's kind of annoying and over-hot, but it really does make the outdoors more bearable. The blood has grown so fetid at this point that breathing outdoors without the respirator feels like inhaling wet rot, and tastes like I imagine a several-day-old carcass would. Not only that, but the mask is an extra layer of protection against accidentally ingesting blood if I were to fall.

A few others lurk here by the playground equipment, but it's clear the main party is farther back in the park. We wade through the murk, between the two baseball diamonds. I can only imagine what they look like now beneath the sea of blood. Just uphill from the diamonds is a forest, and it's at the edge of the trees that the party has been set up.

I'm surprised by the number of people here. From the looks of it, we've got a blend from freshmen to seniors mingling around several kegs of beer.

"How'd they get *those*?" I ask. While beer isn't as in-demand as water, it's in short supply, just like everything else.

Cadence shrugs. "Who cares?"

We push through a group of sophomores in ripped outfits and heavy makeup, toward the cluster of kegs, which are guarded by a couple of lacrosse players. They've decorated the shoulder pads from their uniforms with long metal spikes. Looking around, I start to feel like *I* should have worn spikes, too. My gaze rests on a group of people who've amassed a pile of bones onto a picnic table and are now decorating their costumes with them. One has what appears to be an entire set of ribs attached to his shirt. I shudder and turn away.

The lacrosse guys hand all three of us foamy cups of beer. With straws.

"Nice hair," one of them says to Cadence.

It's too dark to tell, but I'd bet money she's blushing. "Thanks," she says.

And back to the outskirts of the crowd we go, red Solo cups clutched tightly.

"Beer through a straw," says Felix. "Should be interesting."

I maneuver my straw through a corner of my respirator, which I'm pretty sure breaks its seal or whatever—something the respirator's manual considers a bad idea, if I remember correctly—and I'm glad the mask hides my face, because the way I try to hook my tongue around the straw and pull it into my mouth cannot be attractive.

It's weird. Not even the respirator part, but the drinking-beer-through-a-straw part. I almost choke when it fizzes into my mouth, the sour wheat taste of cheap beer bitter on my tongue.

But it's been a long time since I was at a party, even an odd party in a public place with people in costumes and gas masks, and dammit, I'm going to enjoy myself. So I take another sip and another until that fuzzy tinge of tipsiness begins to dull my senses.

"That lacrosse guy was cute, right?" says Cadence, sucking down the rest of her beer. "I'm going to get us more drinks and talk to him."

"Oh, I don't think so." Felix snatches our cups. "If you go, you'll never come back. *I'll* get us more drinks."

"Buzzkill!" Cadence shouts after him. "Literally!"

I laugh.

"Caaaadence! Leaaaa!" Mikayla practically knocks me down with a staggering hug. Her respirator thumps against mine, rattling my cheekbones. Even through the mask, I can smell alcohol on her. Sweating out of her pores.

Cadence and I exchange a look of concern. It's all well and good that she's over giving us the silent treatment (for now), but she's also piss drunk, and to my knowledge, she hasn't spoken to any of us since Felix's peach joke. As selfish as it sounds, I'm not taking care of her tonight.

Felix returns, holding our cups precariously. He barely manages not to spill them when Mikayla lunges for him, all apologies and love.

"It's fine," he says, holding the drinks high over his head. "We're good. Just—could you just . . . Cadence and Lea, your drinks." He says that last part with desperation, because it's clear Mikayla's not listening.

I grab mine, positioning my straw up under my respirator once more. I've got the hang of this now.

"Oh, Cadence, here." Felix dislodges Mikayla from his middle and hands Cadence a piece of paper. "Phone number."

"Are you serious?" Cadence shrieks with delight. "Best wingman ever!"

"Yeah, yeah. You owe me one."

"You guyssss!" Mikayla slurs. "We're not mingling. Let's mingle."

Felix, Cadence, and I have one of those moments where I swear we're speaking to each other telepathically: *Yes, if we mingle, we might escape her.*

So we do. We're drawn into the pulse of the crowd, and it doesn't take long for Mikayla to be distracted away. I don't see Aracely anywhere, and I'm disappointed about that, but this second beer is doing wonderful things for my state of mind.

As we move through the living mass, laughing, chatting, linking, and unlinking, I'm reminded of a documentary I once watched about fire ants. When they felt threatened, the ant colony could form itself into a super-strong, ever-moving structure using just their bodies. They can even float this way, without drowning or becoming dislodged from each other. I bet the fire ants are surviving this bloodpocalypse just fine. Floating across it in their writhing, living bubble.

"I'm getting another drink, want one?" Felix asks loudly, in my ear.

"Not yet, thanks." The fuzz on my brain is getting . . . fuzzier. I don't want to overdo it.

Cadence's enormous fauxhawk fills my view when she throws back her head. She's laughing at a joke I missed. I laugh, too, just for the sake of it.

Then I ask, "How'd you get your hair to stay so well?"

Her hair isn't much longer than mine, but we're still talking at least an eight-inch fauxhawk, not a strand out of place.

"It's a secret." Her voice holds a smile.

"Oh, come on, what is it? Mousse? Super glue? Magic?"

I reach up to touch its spiky ends.

"Don't even think about it!" She laughs, grabbing my hands and holding them tight so I can't reach her hair. I'm giggling, too, and she's sort of leaned on my shoulder, and this is the exact moment I finally see Aracely.

The *worst* moment to see Aracely, because this probably looks kind of bad.

And Aracely sees me, too—she *definitely* sees me. The laughter dies in my throat, replaced with a sort of breathless excitement, because I'd given up hope that I'd see her tonight.

I smile tentatively, even though she probably can't tell through my mask, but then the crowd shifts and she's gone. I want to find her. Say hello. Wander off together into the trees.

I start to move toward where I saw her, but stop short when Cadence's face goes from merry to concerned.

"What?" I ask.

"Look over there. What's happening?"

She gestures behind me. I turn, refocus my attention onto a bunch of people who're starting to get pretty rowdy.

"Drink it! Drink it!" they're chanting.

"They're going to get us all in trouble," I say, annoyed. This isn't someone's basement. We're in a public park, for Christ's sake.

Cadence and I wade toward them, not that I really have a plan here, but *something* has to be done.

It's worse than I could have guessed.

Mikayla stands at the center of a cluster of mostly boys, holding a cup of something that's decidedly not beer.

"Come on, do it!" A girl in ripped leggings goads her. I vaguely recognize the girl. She might be from Mikayla's secondary group of friends. Great friends, clearly.

"But what about the *hair?*" Mikayla's voice is overloud.

Breathy. Slurred. It crackles the speaker in her mask. And she can barely stand.

"It won't go up the straw, don't be a wuss." That's Levi, who I did not expect to see here without Hillary.

Some girl giggles, and while she's not technically touching him, she's pretty damn close and he doesn't seem to be minding it. But no. No, I'm supposed to be giving him the benefit of the doubt, for Hillary's sake. I want us to get back on speaking terms, and being a jerk to Levi won't help.

I return my attention to Mikayla. Wait. Hair. In her cup. She can't possibly . . .

"Oh my God, Mikayla, *no*." I'm rushing toward her before I even realize my feet have moved. "That's fucking gross. Or who even cares about the gross, it's *dangerous*."

I pluck the cup from her unsteady grasp. It's warm. Disgusting. Thick and red. There really is blood in this cup, scooped from the mess at our feet.

"Are *you* going to drink it, then?" Levi. Screw giving him the benefit of the doubt. I should throw this cup at his asshole face. It isn't funny to watch someone who's out-of-their-mind wasted do something this stupid. They're basically asking her to drink a cup full of disease.

"Lea, give it back." Mikayla slumps toward me. Cadence catches her. "I'm going to drink it. Levi dared me."

I curl my hands tighter around the cup, flaring with anger. "He dared you, huh? Well how about *this* for a dare: if Levi drinks half, you'll drink the other half."

Cheers all around at this idea. A strange, mechanical roar of approval. It buzzes through me just like the alcohol did. A cruel smile curves my lips, and I'm glad Levi can't see it. He won't do it; I know he won't. But he's embarrassed now, and that's all I wanted.

His eyes are narrowed, his arms folded. Felix stands right at my side now, in a hovery way, like he's deciding whether to interfere.

"I'll do it," says Levi, "*but.*"

He waits for the cheers to stop before he goes on, "But if I drink the top half, *you* have to drink the rest. Not Mikayla. You."

"Okay." I agree before I can think it over because if I think it over, I'll have to say no. I'm just so mad at him for trying to make a fool of Mikayla in front of everyone, I want to make a fool of *him*, no matter the cost. Plus, the girl next to him has eased away now that he's agreed to this.

"Lea, don't be an idiot." Felix tries to take the cup.

"I don't have to drink anything unless he finishes his half. Which he won't, because only a suicidal person would drink this poison."

Mikayla giggles hysterically at that—I have no idea why. Cadence is struggling to keep her upright. And behind them . . .

Behind them stands Aracely, flanked by a couple of her friends. I can't tell what she thinks of the situation, but she can't be impressed. I wish I could communicate with her somehow, tell her there's no way I'm actually ever going to be so dumb as to drink from that cup, and neither will Levi. I try to tell her with my eyes, but can't stare too long or her friends will notice.

"Here." I hand Levi the cup.

He stares into it for a long moment. I know he's trying

to figure out how to back out and keep his pride. Maybe he's hoping I'll do it for him. Well, he can keep right on hoping.

The party has taken a bad turn; everyone's hushed now, tense with a dark energy. It's a terrible sort of curiosity; you don't *really* want someone to drink something that could damage them in irreparable ways, but at the same time, you do, because what a thing to witness.

He lodges the straw beneath his respirator and takes a deep pull.

I can't believe it. I *caused* this. Reflexively, I reach out to stop him from drinking more, because Jesus. But he gags and I jump back, almost not in time.

He barely gets the mask off before puking. And puking and puking.

With feigned nonchalance, I poke Felix in the ribs. "Told you. I don't have to drink a thing." And now I'm laughing, nearly as hard as Mikayla, who still hasn't stopped. The crowd is roaring, too. I wonder if their laughter masks the same sort of hysteria as mine. I can't believe he did that. *Why* would he do that? Why didn't I stop him sooner? I truly thought he wouldn't drink it, but maybe I shouldn't have pushed him into this corner. I feel sick thinking about it.

Felix shakes his head. "You are such a jerk." But he says it with affection. "Hill's going to be so mad when she hears about this."

That part's soberingly true. What's done is done. But she's really not going to forgive me easily for this one. Nor should she.

"Lea, can you help me here?" Cadence still struggles with

Mikayla. "I'm going to walk her home; just help me get her away from everyone."

I sling one of Mikayla's arms around my shoulder and help guide her away from the crowd. "Are you sure you've got her?" I ask. "I can walk her home with you."

"Nah, it's on my way anyhow. I've got her."

I watch them go. Mikayla and Cadence live on the same street. It *is* out of my way, but I feel bad about leaving Cadence alone to do drunk duty.

"Lea!" Felix rushes toward me. "You've gotta get out of here."

"Why?"

"Levi's done puking, and now he says he's going to drink the rest so you'll have to."

I cross my arms. "Are you fucking serious? It's poison and he knows it. God, if he actually keeps any of it down . . . I've got to stay, I have to make him stop."

"Goddammit, Lea, don't be an idiot. You know if you go back over there, it'll only make things worse."

"Then I'll . . ." I trail off because Cadence and Mikayla are already too far away, swallowed by darkness.

"Go into the woods. I'll say you had to piss. Just get out of here. Okay?" He's shoving me toward the trees, his hands painful-tight on my shoulders. "I'll take care of the rest."

"Okay! I'm going," I grumble. Through the mask, it translates as incoherent babble. I don't want to leave like this—Hillary will be mad enough as it is—but Felix is probably right. If I stay, things could escalate.

I'm barely into the trees when there's a voice at my shoulder.

"Hey," Aracely whispers.

I smile. She's wearing a skirt that looks like she might've fashioned it out of actual rags, and a shirt that's tied together rather than buttoned. It leaves a couple inches of her stomach bare, and pushes her cleavage up so that it's hard to keep my eyes from straying there. She looks like a post-apocalyptic queen.

Her hand slips into mine, and right now, I think I would follow her anywhere. Screw Levi.

We weave through the trees until we're far enough in that we're unlikely to be interrupted by someone desperate to pee or to make out or to puke in private.

"So what was that about?" Aracely asks. "Do I even want to know?"

"Probably not. I just wanted him to look foolish. I know that's awful."

"He seems like a dick. No judgment from me."

"He's Hillary's boyfriend. She's already pissed at me. This'll make it so much worse."

"I'm sorry." She takes my hand and pulls me closer. "You were never going to drink it, though, right?"

"No! No, of course not."

"Good." She brushes fingertips down my cheek. "Because I was ready to stop you if you tried."

"How very knight-in-shining-armor of you."

"I would never wear armor. Imagine how hot you'd be inside all that metal. Plus, I think to be a really great knight, I'd need a horse, and I'm not so sure my building allows horses."

"Yeah, it'd be awfully hard to get it to go up and down all those stairs. Wait, can they even walk down stairs?"

"I don't know. I think that's just cows?"

"Maybe." I tilt my head, trying to imagine horses *or* cows going down stairs.

Aracely pulls her phone from a hidden pocket in her skirt. "I have to know," she says. Then, after a few seconds, "Dammit, no Internet here."

"An unanswerable mystery," I say.

"Unanswerable, please. I'm going to look it up when I go home."

"Dork."

She grins unapologetically. "Like you're not."

And then, sirens. Both our heads snap toward the sound like we're startled deer.

"Shit!" Aracely squeezes my hand.

"We'll have to go out the back of the woods. Maybe up past the school?"

She nods. We slosh through the trees, toward someone's backyard, in the opposite direction of the flashing police lights. A muted terror fights against the haze over my thoughts. I've never been at a party that got busted by the police.

"Another car! Do you see it?" I pull Aracely up short at the tree line.

So we have to edge around the woods, take a longer route back to Main Street. This would be hard enough on a regular night, but with hair catching around our ankles and bones tripping us every other step, it feels like a marathon.

"I hope all our friends got away," Aracely says. "Shit, I kind of abandoned everyone when I saw you."

"Me, too." I'm pretty sure Cadence and Mikayla were well out of the way before the police arrived, but Felix . . .

Instinctively, my hand goes to my pants pocket, but my phone isn't there. Crap, I forgot it at home. I hope he's not trying to get hold of me.

We reach Aracely's corner, and she pulls me inside her building. "Just for a minute," she says.

I lift my respirator free of my face. The air feels cold on my nose and mouth after the hot moisture of my own breath. Aracely has dark red lines where the edges of her mask pressed. I trace one from the bridge of her nose down her cheek. And then our lips meet in an unconscious moment of perfectly synchronized movement. I press her into the wall next to the stairwell, my fingers in her hair, and her arms tight around me. We don't have long and this isn't very private, so this is not a soft or sweet sort of kiss. It's intense and hot and aching. It's teeth nipping lips and nails scratching skin. It would lead somewhere more, if we weren't barely concealed in a public stairwell. Our hips are pressed together and I'm very aware of the bareness of her legs under her tiny skirt.

I let go of her because I have to. My hands linger at her waist, thumbs skimming the bare skin below the hem of her shirt.

"We should sneak out again some night," I say when I've caught my breath. "Just us."

"For sure," Aracely agrees.

And for a moment, we both just stand there. I fight the urge to kiss her again. It takes all my willpower to slowly replace the respirator over my face and walk out the door. I thought it was bad at school, when I only got to see her some-times. But this is so much worse, when I see her barely ever.

I miss her the moment I step out the door, and I would turn right back around except I'm nervous that police might still be patrolling the area, scouting for stray teens. And I'm sort of dizzy; not really drunk, but I was buzzed enough for a while there that between sobering up and battling exhaustion, I feel disoriented and ill.

Water and blood sloshes wildly beneath me as I cross the bridge. I don't look down. I wouldn't be able to see much anyway, not in the dark, but the high, thrashing water unnerves me nonetheless.

It feels like a century before I've reached my house. I'm bone-tired from slogging through the sludge, and all I can think about is sleep. I slide back in through my window, flailing gracelessly onto my bed, but keep my feet dangling outside until I can yank off my bloodstained boots.

I'll have to clean them somehow, before my parents see them. I wish I'd thought of that earlier. I'm too exhausted. I'll shove them in the closet and deal with them tomorrow.

I turn, stumble to my feet, and freeze.

Mom and Dad stand in my doorway, arms identically folded.

I am in so much trouble.

16.

"What were you *thinking*?"

"Is that alcohol on your breath?"

"How could you *do* that to us? We were so worried!"

"You went out *in the dark*, knowing *full well* how dangerous it would be if you fell?"

"We thought we could trust you!"

"What happened to the girl we raised?"

"We called you and called you, and you didn't even have
the decency to answer your phone!"

They've cycled through these same screeches of anger and
disappointment for nearly a half hour now, while I cower,
cornered on my bed. I tried interrupting at first, but I've
given up on that. They don't care what I have to say. So I've
started to tune them out. I focus instead on inching my phone
deeper beneath my pillow, hiding it in case they decide to
take it.

And when silence replaces their outrage, I don't notice
right away. Not until Mom's impatient, *"Well?"*

What was it she asked? I sift through my brain. Oh, right.
What do you have to say for yourself, young lady?

"How did you know I'd left?" Wrong response, I know.
I'm an idiot.

Both of their faces harden identically. "Felix's mother
called looking for him," Mom explains tightly.

That's bad.

"I'm sorry I snuck out," I say grudgingly. "But no one
gets to see each other now that school's closed, so—"

"Do not even *try* that with us," Mom snarls. "You were

very, *very* wrong to do this, and you know it. You could have been hurt. You could have been *killed*. Do you even understand how dangerous it was, what you did? I'm taking your computer, and I'm taking your phone. Where is it?"

She unplugs my laptop from its power cord and holds it to her chest, lips tightened into a line. Thank God for my foresight.

"I dropped it somewhere, I think. I had it when I left, but then I tried to call Felix on my way home, and it was gone." This will make them angrier, but it will buy me a little longer with my precious communication.

Mom's nostrils flare. "Well, you're not getting a new one for a very long time."

I don't say anything. There's no point in protesting.

"We're going to have to do something about your window," says Dad. "But not tonight."

I bite my tongue to keep from speaking. Maybe if I'm contrite, they won't do it.

"We are *very* disappointed in you," he adds.

"Sorry," I whisper.

"We'll discuss this further in the morning," Mom tells me. "Go to bed."

And they both slam out of my room. I lie on my stomach, pressing my face into my pillow. This is the *worst*. Now I won't be able to sneak out to see Aracely. I won't be able to sneak out to do *anything*. It's just me, my bedroom, my parents. That is my whole world now.

My phone buzzes beneath my pillow. No name's listed, but I know who it is. Felix has a secret cell phone, one of those no-plan ones you can get at Walmart. His mom takes his other one away at least once a month.

"Hey," I whisper. "In trouble, I'm guessing?"

"Yeah. You, too? My mom said she called Hillary's parents and then yours. Sorry."

"They told me. After they yelled for a while."

"Shitty."

"Yeah. Did Cadence and Mikayla make it home okay, too? Do you know?"

"Yeah, they did. Cadence's parents didn't notice anything, of course. And Mom never called them."

"That's good." Though a less nice part of me kind of wishes she had. Misery loving company, I guess.

"Hey, who was that girl you went into the woods with?"

Crap. "I went into the woods because you told me to."

"Yeah but you were talking to that girl on the way. Who was she?"

"Oh, that's Aracely. She lives on my way to school, so I see her sometimes. We were just talking for a second, is all." I hold my breath. Please believe my half-lie, *please*.

"So . . . you guys were talking, or, you know, *talking*?" His voice is oozing with over-interest. I'm going to have to seriously divert him.

"Oh, come on, Felix. I've told you who every single lesbian is in the whole school."

"So then . . . you could introduce me to her. Right?"

This I did not see coming. For half a beat, I consider saying no, but you know what, this might actually make things easier, in a way. So long as he forgets this conversation before school restarts. "Sure, of course."

"Awesome. I didn't see her up close, but she looked pretty cute."

"'Pretty cute' is an understatement," I say without thinking. God, what is *wrong* with me?

"*In*teresting. So you have a crush, then."

Silence. I should deny it. I can't bring myself to.

"Forget the introducing thing," he says.

"What? Why?"

"Because . . . you never know. If you like someone, I'm not going to get in the middle of it, whether there's a chance for you or not. It's that old saying, right? Bros before hos!"

I suppress a snort of laughter into my pillow. "Did you just call me your *bro*?"

"Hey, I can only be so sentimental. Take what you can get."

"Well, I—" Footsteps in the hallway. I whisper-hiss, "Parents! I have to go. Talk to you later."

My phone is under my pillow and my head atop it, eyes closed, before the footsteps reach my room.

I think it's Dad. The breathing as he stands over me sounds masculine. I keep mine as steady as possible, praying he'll believe I'm asleep. He stands there for a long, long while, but finally the thump of footsteps mark his departure, as does the gentle click of my door closing behind him.

Alone at last. Alone, but not free.

This is my prison. I close my eyes tighter and remember what it felt like to have Aracely's mouth pressed to mine, because I'm going to have to make that memory tide me over for a long, long while.

17.

I am giving my parents the silent treatment. For two days, I've vacillated between shame at how childish the silent treatment is, and righteous indignation at how unfair it is for them to cut me off from the entire world. Because that's exactly what they did. Dad got plywood from work and they nailed it over my whole window. My room feels like a cave now.

The only positive is that Mom let me keep my phone after she discovered it yesterday. She *meant* to take it, but I temporarily broke my silence and begged with such shamelessness that she probably thought I'd lose my shit if she didn't let me have it.

I've kept myself glued to the phone ever since, to this tiny square of plastic that is my only connection to the outside world. I glance anxiously at it now, trying to convince myself not to make another phone call. Because I'm not the only one giving the silent treatment. Hillary is mad as hell about what happened between Levi and me. She told me as much via a terse text message, and I haven't gotten her to communicate with me since. I cave and call her, for what has to be the seventieth time this morning.

"*What?*"

It startles me so much to hear her finally answer, I nearly drop my phone. "Please hear me out," I beg.

She sighs heavily. "I'm listening."

"Look I *know* you told me to give him the benefit of the doubt, and I *know* I didn't, but he was being so mean to Mikayla. If you'd been there, you would have seen. He was, like, actively cruel to her."

"Maybe it was good for her. She's manipulative and, how did you say it? *Actively cruel*, all the time."

"I know. And if she'd been sober, or even a little sober, I would say yeah, she deserved it. But you can't do something like that to a person who's so out of their mind, they don't even know what's going on. So . . . so I'm sorry. I'm really and truly sorry, but I just, I had been drinking, too, and I shouldn't have done that to Levi; I should have let someone else step in and stop the whole thing, but I couldn't."

"That's not even the worst part, though. You made my boyfriend drink blood. You taunted him in front of everyone, he said, and you let him do that, and then you *left*. That's so shitty, Lea." Her voice is so filled with hurt, each word is like a pinprick in my stomach.

"He has free will, though. I swear I never meant for him to drink it. And I definitely didn't mean to abandon him. I left because—" *Because Felix told me to.* It's on the tip of my tongue but no. Felix was just being a good friend. I can't throw him under the bus to save myself. That's unfair. "The police. I went into the trees to pee, and then I heard sirens and I ran."

Silence.

"Look, Hillary. Seriously. I never, *ever* thought he would actually drink it. I mean, come on!"

"So? Does that really make a difference?"

She's right. "I know I did a shitty thing. But so did Levi. Can you at least tell me you know he did, too?"

"Of course I know that. Of course." Sniffling. She's crying. "God, you are both such assholes."

"Maybe that's the problem," I say, hoping to cheer her up. "Maybe we're just both assholes in the same way, and it makes it harder for us to get along."

It works. She laughs. "You're so full of shit."

I sink onto my bed. "I'll try with him. I know I promised before, but if Levi will promise to try with me, then I promise to try with him, too. If I ever get to leave my house again, anyway."

"Okay. I believe you." She pauses. "So I guess I missed quite the party, huh?"

"Yeah, apocalypse costumes and blood drinking and police breaking it up. Actually, a lot of the costumes were pretty cool. And Cadence got some lacrosse player's phone number. I'm guessing Levi didn't get caught? And . . . and he's okay, right?"

"Nah, he got home safe. I think they just grabbed a few people and called it good. And yeah, he's okay."

"How come you stayed home?"

"My parents have been keeping extra weird hours because things are a mess at the hospital. I had to stay home with Finn. Good thing, too, since Felix's mom called."

"Seriously. My parents were waiting in my room for me when I got back. I'm basically imprisoned forever now."

Imprisoned forever. Suddenly, my lungs can't get enough air. It's like all the oxygen has been sucked from my room. My room, which is not big enough to sit in alone, day after day.

My room, which is . . . which is *bleeding*?

"Hillary, I have to go." I say it quickly and don't wait before hanging up and scrambling back, pressing myself against the wall.

There is blood. On my floor. Seeping up, up through the carpet like crimson beads of sweat. It crawls over everything. A thick red stain encircling the legs of my chair, reaching toward the edges of my bed skirt.

A roar pounds in my ears. Shrill, sharp screaming. It's me, I'm screaming.

Mom bursts into my room. "What is it? Lea, what's wrong?"

I point a trembling finger at the floor, but it's gone. There's nothing. No blood, no stain, nothing to indicate there ever *was* any blood.

"I . . . there was blood, I saw . . . I don't know. I'm fine." Except I collapse into a sobbing, shaking mess, and it's very clear that I am, in fact, the opposite of fine.

Mom sits beside me and strokes my hair. "Shh, Lea, it's all right. You're safe. You're all right."

She thinks I'm losing it. I know she does. She tells me all the time how safe I am, and how she's going to protect me. I have nightmares almost daily, and now I'm hallucinating blood.

Maybe I *am* losing it.

I don't know what's real anymore.

"Sweetie." Her fingers move more slowly through my hair now. "The day you got your respirator, did you—"

"Mom," I groan. "Not again. *No.* I didn't get blood in my mouth or my eyes or anywhere dangerous. I swear. Don't you think I'd know? Don't you think I'd tell you?"

"Of course. Of course."

We sit in silence for a few long moments while I battle a choking fear that maybe I *did* ingest blood, somehow, and I just don't remember. Could it do that? Make me forget? I shudder at the thought. Mom squeezes an arm tightly around my shoulders.

"I will do anything I have to, to keep you safe," she whispers. "Anything."

A chill crawls up my spine. A slow crawl, like it wants me to fully appreciate the fear Mom's words invoke.

"You don't have to do anything," I say hoarsely. "I'm okay, really. I'm just a little stir crazy is all."

Mom rubs my back soothingly, like she did when I was a child. "I know you are, and I'm sorry. But you really are safer this way."

"Why? Dad's still going to work every day. Lots of people are."

She doesn't answer. It's that thing again, where she knows I won't like what she says, so she says nothing at all. What's she keeping secret from me? I'm not stupid. I've noticed the worsened smell, even indoors. I've read news reports on the Internet, watched them on TV. People are going crazy, dangerously crazy, and we have no idea if it's curable. Water and food are in short supply. News outlets—or, more likely, the government—are trying to spin it like people are figuring something out, but who actually thinks that's true, at this point?

But I want to go out there. I want to see people. My friends. Aracely. Hell, I'd even spend an afternoon bonding with Levi for something to do.

"Please, Mom," I whisper. "Please let me go somewhere. Anywhere."

"We haven't been stuck indoors for that long, sweetheart. You're going to have to get used to it. It won't be forever. I promise."

Her face clouds, and she stands abruptly, and I think I'm not the only one who's going crazy.

"Are you going to be okay now?" she asks.

I nod.

She kisses my forehead and leaves me alone. I eye the floor warily, because the blood was so real. I could smell it, taste it. But when I brush my fingertips over my carpet, it's as plush as ever. No crispness from dried blood. No residual damp.

"You are not going to go insane," I tell myself sternly. "You. Are. Not."

I have to do something. Something normal, to cleanse my brain. The Internet. Mom still has my laptop. I could try and get it back now, maybe, but I've lost interest in it all anyway. Everything these days is about the blood, and I don't want to think about the blood. I want sanity.

An idea strikes me. I reach under my bed for the shoe box I keep there, filled with my old, angsty diaries from when I was a kid. Those are always fun. The box slides out easily, dusty from being abandoned under there for so long. I brush it off and lift it up. When I do, an old receipt or something unsticks from its underside and floats to the ground.

I set the box on my bed and crouch beside the receipt, my jaw hanging open.

Carefully, I pick it up by the corner, with only my fore-finger and thumb.

Everything else on the floor is pristine, normal. But this receipt . . .

It is stained red.

Red with dried blood.

18.

Mom returns my laptop in the morning. Then we sit down—as a family, because Dad has the day off—and discuss safety measures and regulation of our water intake and precautions to take against potential looters, and it all feels like I'm having an informational brochure read to me.

"Get your respirator," Dad says when it's over.

I do as I'm told. Dad gets his, too, and Mom ties a scarf over her mouth and nose.

"Where are we going?" I ask.

"Home Depot," says Mom.

"Why? Isn't it closed?"

"Lea." Dad shakes his head at me. Great, so now I can't even ask simple questions.

When I step out onto the porch, I feel almost panicked. I wanted to come outside more than anything, and it feels so good, so free and unclaustrophobic, but it has gotten so bad out here. The blood is all-consuming: splashed onto fences and telephone poles and the sides of houses. There's hair dangling from tree branches and wires. Stray bones sitting on the steps to people's houses. It's all so wrong, yet sweeping my eyes over everything, I have this deep sense of rightness that disturbs me to my very core.

Mom takes my hand as we walk down the steps to Dad's truck, and I try to calm down.

A spray of red follows us as Dad backs out of the driveway and heads down the street. It's like driving through a brook.

Cottage Street is heavy with traffic. The interstate is

worse. Some cars appear to be stuck. Others are honking and revving impatiently. Mom taps her nails against the dash while we sit in a gridlock, until Dad says, "Fuck this," and drives along the breakdown lane.

"Steve!" Mom hisses, gripping the handle on the glove box like it's a steering wheel.

I know better than to openly take sides here, but honestly I'm just glad we're moving.

"Where are all these people going?" I ask. Basically, nothing's open anymore. Only vital stuff. Hospitals. Electricity. The food and water center set up at the post office.

Dad shrugs. "Walmart. Shaws. Canada."

I snort. "Canada?"

Another shrug. "People get all sorts of ideas during crises. You never know."

Meadow Street is better than the interstate, but not by much. We have to circle the Home Depot parking lot several times before a spot opens up. It's surreal. Especially since, like I thought, it's not open.

I steel myself for a repeat of the grocery store. I may be small, but I still have my pocketknife. If anything happens in there, I'm ready.

"Should we be doing this?" I ask as we approach the building. This feels very wrong. We're looting. We are about to go steal things as a family like that's just what people do.

"Don't worry about it," says Dad, and I want to throat-punch him for being so condescending.

We step through broken doors, crunch across shattered glass that's lodged in the mat of hair. The blood has seeped in here some, but by the interior set of doors it's just a thin layer and the glass shards poke out, giving it the look of a crime scene.

It's probably just as dangerous. Getting cut by bloody glass can't be good whether the toxins get in that way or not.

The interior lighting is nonexistent, because of course electricity is shut off to places that don't need it right now, but the store is *filled* with people. Many carry flashlights and torches and other battery-powered lighting devices they probably stole straight from the store. The upper reaches of the warehouse-like building are swallowed by shadow, its high shelves looming.

Shelves are broken, items scattered. The aisle with all the lamps glitters with broken glass. Upturned carts block the floor. Lights bob down the aisles like the glow-in-the-dark lures of deep-sea predators. Looters wield their goods like weapons. I'm nearly beheaded by a piece of timber. I sidestep a skull that must've gotten kicked inside somehow.

I pass tons of people I know as we head for the lumber section. Freshman twins who live on my street, dragging their parents to the exit. One of Aracely's friends, looking lost. I almost wave to him, but remember he has no idea who I am.

And Felix, who gets my attention by poking me in the arm. He's wearing his respirator, too. I almost don't recognize him with half his face covered, and the rest of him shadowy behind lantern light.

"What're *your* parents here for?" he asks in his robot voice.

"Plywood and stuff. How about your mom?"

"Same."

"Lea!" Mom snaps her fingers at me like I'm a dog.

"I'll catch up," I say sharply.

"No, it's okay," says Felix. "My mom's getting ready to leave, so I better go."

"Okay. See you."

He waves at me while dodging crazed looters. I watch him until he disappears, the lanky frame of this person who's so familiar to me. Who I've spent so much time with over the years. I said *see you* like it's a weekend and we'll be together in AP psych on Monday. But we won't. Mom won't let me out. She won't let me invite people over, and we're about to close off the whole house the way they already did my window. When *will* I see him—or anyone?

I miss all my friends—and Aracely—with a hunger that gnaws. It's barely been any time at all, and already I'm so lonesome, it's like I've been in isolation for years. I even miss Mikayla, and I'm used to going weeks without talking to her.

Someone grabs me tightly by the upper arm. It's Dad.

"We need to get out of here now," he says. He and Mom each have one of those huge carts you drag along behind you. They're stacked high with plywood.

I nearly slip in a puddle of blood on the way past the cash registers. I catch myself on the plywood on Mom's cart. It tears my hand. A long, deep scratch against my palm. Neither of my parents see it happen, so I just ball my hand into a fist and pretend the stinging doesn't hurt.

A woman crouches near the doors, sobbing and trembling. She's older, with her steel-gray hair cut short and neat. Thick glasses magnify her tears, and I want to hug her.

"Are you all right?" I ask.

She looks up at me, startled. Has no one else asked? Has

no one thought she might need help?

"I'm fine, dear," she chokes out. A smudge of blood mars one of her cheeks.

I open my mouth to say more, but Dad's pulling me along again.

"She's scared," he tells me while we load the truck. "A store like that isn't the place for someone like her right now."

"Someone like what?" I ask. My respirator masks the shake in my voice. "Nice? Elderly?"

Dad hugs me, tightly, unexpectedly. "I'm sorry, Lea," he says. "I'm sorry about all of this."

Then he lets me go and we pile back into the truck. While they're both watching the road, I open my fist between my knees. The cut doesn't look too deep, but it's long and my whole hand is smeared with blood.

Now I let myself feel the sting. Tilt my hand sideways and watch the crimson droplets well slowly and fall onto the floor.

Hammering keeps me up all night. I guess it doesn't matter—I have nowhere to go—but it's still incredibly aggravating.

At about three a.m., I give up on tossing and turning in my bed. I throw off my covers and stomp across my room.

But I pause at the end of the hallway, because Mom and Dad are talking while they work. Dad's telling Mom some story about how they're keeping the hair from clogging the dam, and she's listening, responding, engaging.

It's so unfamiliar to me now; their voices bring back feelings of my early childhood.

Maybe this is what's *really* happening. The earth isn't trying to kill us; it's trying to unite us. What other explanation is there for the way my parents seem to have become warmer toward each other? It's been so long since they tried, and now here they are, having a good conversation in our living room.

I creep back to my bedroom. I don't want to interrupt whatever's going on out there.

I stare at my window even though it isn't really a window anymore. A dog yips somewhere in the distance. It's strange how rarely I hear or see animals anymore. I read an article about how they're dying of thirst, or else retreating in that mysterious way animals do, surviving in little pockets of sanctuary humans will never find. I don't know what people are doing with their pets. Keeping them safe, I hope.

My eyelids are heavy with sleep, but there's just no way, not with all the pounding and sawing. I close my eyes and try to picture myself somewhere else. A beach or something. It doesn't work—all I can see are bleeding waves.

So I lose myself in my memories. Childhood memories: playing at the beach, learning to ride a bike, lying in the hammock in our tiny backyard and reading books I'd picked out myself from the library. I was Finn's age then, eight or maybe nine. Hillary and I used to meet at the library because our parents didn't want either of us to walk all the way to the other's house, but they were okay with us going that far. Sometimes other kids met us there, too, and we played hide-and-seek in the stacks, which did not amuse the librarians at all. Hillary would always get embarrassed when they scolded us, but she'd always buckle under peer pressure the next time, and do it all over.

I wonder if Finn will get the chance to do normal stuff like that with his friends, or if he'll be stuck in this bloody future where we live like islands, isolated and broken. I hate the very thought. Why can't I just have my memories; why do they have to be tainted by my fear for the future?

Restlessly, I pad back to the living room. "Want help?" I ask.

Both parents turn to me with soft expressions on their faces.

"That would be wonderful," says Mom.

Dad hands me a hammer and some nails. "Just pound them in around the edges," he says, holding on to a monstrous piece of plywood covering the picture window in our living room.

We work all through the night, hammering, sawing, strength-testing the wood. The three of us: a family united.

19.

Isolation is miserable.

At night, I dream of blood. Different dreams, always. But always, I wake in fear and sweat, gripping my sheets in my fists.

Tonight, the blood dribbles steadily onto my forehead from a leak in the ceiling. *Drip. Drip. Drip.* Each drop sizzles on my skin, sinking deeper than the last. I can't move, can't even turn my head. All I can do is watch the beads of blood break free from the ceiling, feel them burn my flesh, deeper and deeper, carving a divot into my skull. Until finally, one burns right through the bone into my brain.

And then I'm up with a gasp, unsticking hair from the side of my sweaty face.

I scoot away from my pillow and glance warily up at the ceiling. Nothing. There's nothing dripping onto me. No leak. Just the *tick, tick, tick* of the clock, and me, losing my fucking mind.

I rip my clock off the wall, because it's the ticking that was doing it, manifesting itself in my nightmare. I claw out its batteries and throw it at my door for good measure.

It breaks with a satisfying crack of cheap plastic. Pieces fly everywhere. I sink back onto my bed, hugging my knees.

It's not even fifteen seconds later that my parents knock on my door.

"Lea," Dad calls. "Everything all right?"

"I'm fine."

He opens the door and turns on my light. All three of us cringe from it like underground-dwelling mammals forced into sunlight.

"My clock was bothering me," I explain when they both stare confoundedly at the broken pieces on the floor.

Dad just sort of blinks at me, and Mom doesn't even try to comprehend. She shuffles back down the hallway.

"Next time," Dad mumbles, turning to follow suit, "take out the batteries."

"I did," I tell the closed door.

They probably think I'm crazy. But it's not me who's crazy. I'm not the one boarding this place up like it's a fucking fallout shelter.

Except there it is again, that gnawing worry that somehow the blood got into my system, that I *am* crazy. Or that trace amounts in our drinking water from before the warning were enough to mess me up. I squeeze my fist, poking a finger against the healing cut from Home Depot. I've been careful, but was I careful enough? What if I have more cuts, ones I don't know about and didn't find during one of my checks?

But no. No, it's normal to feel like this. It's normal to have nightmares when you're barricaded into your home, when your waking hours are nightmare enough already. It's normal to worry that the blood got to me somehow, like the way you feel as if something's on you when there's a spider in your room and it escapes before you can kill it.

I pick up my phone to check the time and somehow end up texting Aracely.

This sucks.

I regret it immediately. I would hate anyone who texted me at three fifteen in the morning. But my phone soon beeps with a reply:

I know. I miss you. And real life.

Tears burn unexpectedly in my eyes.

I miss you too. And the sun. I feel like a vampire.

If you were a vampire, you'd be having a great time I bet.

Then, before I can even reply: *Sorry. Terrible joke.*

I smile. It wasn't a terrible joke. It was a great one. I text her that.

For forty-five minutes, we text back and forth. About small things, big things, silly things. I tell her about my nightmares, and she tells me about hers. I tell her about the time Felix put gum in my hair in sixth grade, and I had to be sent to the nurse's office to get it cut out. She tells me about the time her friend Marina's little sister snuck up behind her and took a big chunk out of her hair with scissors. When we finally say good night, I feel calmer. And when I fall asleep this time, it's not blood I dream of.

It's better things.

20.

Time has lost all meaning.

Our house is a fortress of plywood and nails. Every window is covered. Our front door has twelve locks. Most of our water is in the spare room. It has more locks than the front door, and the keys are hidden all over the house like a game of Clue.

Dad got me a can of Mace for my bedside. In case.

Dad still goes to work. Some people do. Pretending life is normal. Mom stays home with me. She scrubs our entry with a dry mop, which just makes it pink.

I nap. And eat precise amounts of food. And drink precise amounts of water. And use a toilet that swirls with crimson water and clogs at least three times daily because of the hair or a tiny bone that works its way into the plumbing. And I nap some more. Text my friends, listen to emergency broadcasts, press my nose to the boards covering my window. Try not to have nightmares.

Watch the world slowly fall apart.

21.

I have been in this house forever.

That's what it feels like, anyway. The days are long when nothing is happening. Nothing, and everything. I sit at my computer, idly scrolling through the headlines on CNN.

Heavy piles of hair on power lines cause widespread power outages

Treetop-dwelling tribes in Papua New Guinea: Have they had the right idea all along?

Hospitals overflowing with patients suffering varied and severe forms of blood-induced psychosis

All air travel officially suspended worldwide; stranded travelers afraid and upset

Photos: Nature, before and after the blood

I've read all of these and more. The newest headline is five days old. I think. I'm starting to lose track of days a little. Regardless, updates via the news are becoming sparser and sparser. It's like at some point over the past few days, we just gave up. All of us, the whole world. Officially, I think we're supposed to believe someone's still researching this. And hell, maybe they are. Maybe the world's brightest scientific minds are throwing everything they've got into their research. But at this point, it's a lost cause. We all know that. It'll end or it won't. For now, all we can do is ride it out, tough as that is.

It's too hard for people to go to work in these conditions. Stores, businesses, day cares, schools; they're all closed. Hospitals and other essential buildings are still in operation, but not at full staff. Doctors and nurses and police officers and firemen are on call always but aren't doing their usual hours. Dad's still working, too, because the electricity the dam provides is more important than ever. His days are longer than they've ever been. Sometimes it's twelve hours or more before we see him in the evening.

He's the only one who leaves our house anymore. I sit in my room, and Mom compulsively measures the water levels in all our buckets, and how much gas we've got in all the tanks we're storing in the same room now. She takes her Bible out, puts it away. Takes it out again. Tells me she's more convinced than ever that God is a sham . . . and then holes up in her room highlighting Bible passages. I wish I could help her with her crisis of faith, but I don't even know what *I* believe.

I brush my fingertips over my phone. Stare at the computer screen again. Breathe deeply for the familiar resisting sensation of my respirator.

I wear it all the time now. It's safer that way.

The blood calls to me. It sings a song that runs threads through my veins and tugs me to the window. Sometimes I blink and I am there and I have no idea how long my nose has been pressed against those boards or what lured me in the first place.

The respirator, somehow, makes this happen less often.

My computer trills; the alert I set up for when Aracely gets online. Bunches of cell towers are down now, so depending on the provider, some people have no reception anymore. My phone is fine, but Aracely's isn't. The Internet is our only communication, and even that is pretty patchy.

Her: *hey*

Me: *hey :)*

Her: *Doing all right?*

Me: *Kinda. You?*

Her: *I'm still sane. I think. So there's that.*

We have nothing else to say. We've already talked about everything, it feels like. Our childhoods. Our sexuality. Our relationship. Our friends and families. I know more about her than all the other girls I've dated, combined. I know that her favorite color is pink, but not just any pink; it's the exact shade that uses the HTML code FF6699. She looked it up once, she told me, because she thought that saying one's favorite color was pink seemed very inexact. And I know that while she knows all sorts of things about how to fix cars, she's so terrible at actually driving them that her dad's making her wait until she's eighteen to get her license. "For the safety of humanity," she told me his exact words were. I know her biggest fears and her deepest secrets. And she knows mine, too. She's told me about the moment she knew she liked girls, when one of her friends got hold of an issue of *Playboy* and showed it to her. "So cliché," she told me. "That's how, like, *everyone* learns they like girls."

Maybe there's lots we should be able to say to each other now, with all this knowledge, but sometimes your heart is just so heavy and your loneliness so sharp that words are lost altogether.

Her: *Shit, my dad says I have to get offline for a while. Sorry.*

Me: *It's ok. I'll ttyl!*

Her: *ok. Miss you!*

And she's gone.

I close my eyes. When I open them, I'm at the window. My respirator is jammed against my face, digging painfully into my nose and pushing uncomfortably on the bar in my lip. I've dug my nails into the edges of the plywood, like maybe I was trying to pry it free. One of them has broken off and is bleeding. I pull off my respirator and suck on my bleeding fingertip to stop the flow. It tastes coppery and I like it, and that disturbs me.

It's time to give up on my lip piercing for now, I think, so I unscrew the ball on the end and pull out the bar. I set it in its box with my others, and poke at the empty spot on the inside of my lip with my tongue. It feels very strange. But it'll make the respirator less uncomfortable, and that's the important thing right now.

There's a pounding coming from the living room. I hop off my bed to go investigate.

It's Mom, nailing plywood.

Over the front door.

"Uh, Mom?" I say hesitantly. "Dad's still not home, is he?"

"No."

She hammers the next nail with a force that can only be

fueled by rage. I get an ill, shaky feeling in my stomach.

"Well . . . where is he?"

Mom sets down her hammer and turns to face me.

"I don't know," she says. "I've been calling him, but . . . nothing."

"He's probably on his way. Why would you block up the door?"

She stops what she's doing and just stares at me. "He was supposed to be home two days ago. I really don't think he's on his way."

"Two days ago?" I furrow my brow and glance at the clock. "No, more like two *hours* ago. He left this morning. He's probably just delayed again."

"This morning?" Now it's Mom's turn to look confused. "Sweetheart, I think you're losing track of time."

"One of us is," I say slowly. "But I don't think it's me."

Her grip loosens on the hammer, but only for a second. "No," she says. "It's you. I'm sure of it."

"I don't . . ." I'm not sure, suddenly. *Has* it been two days? Every hour, every minute, every second feels so agonizingly long, and then there are those moments where I lose track altogether and I'm pressed to the window, and other than the clock, I don't know what's day and what's night anymore. "We could look at your phone. See the times and dates of your calls to him."

"Okay." She hands it to me.

But her phone isn't like mine. It's older, simpler. It condenses her calls, so all I know is that she's called Dad forty-one times, but I don't know when or for how long.

"So?" she asks nervously.

"I can't tell."

Her lips thin into a grim line. "I'm positive that I'm not wrong, Lea. I really am."

I swallow hard, my throat dry. Two days. How did I lose that much time? *How?* Or did she? Just because she's confident doesn't mean she's right. Does it?

"I still don't think you should block the door," I whisper.

Mom twists the hammer in her hands, and something dangerous glints in her eyes. Something that makes me want to hide. "We'll be safer this way. It's going to be all right."

She makes as though to cup my face in her hands, but I flinch away. I've *never* flinched away from my mother, and immediately I regret it.

Her hands fall to her sides, her eyes sad and wide. "Are you frightened of me?"

Am I? "No, of course not. I don't know why I did that."

She wrings her hands. I know she wants to reach for me again—test if I'm being honest—but I don't thinks she wants to risk it.

"I would never let anything happen to you," she says. "I hope you know that."

I nod and try to smile. God, I wish she would stop saying that.

When she returns to her work on the door, I return to my room. I mean to text Hillary to talk about this since she, at least, still has cell service. But the pounding reverberates against my skull. The rhythmic tap of metal on metal, slowly closing me in. So it isn't Hillary I text. It's Dad.

Please come home, I type. *I'm scared.*

PSA

Power Outage Hotline

If the power goes out in your home, please call the newly created National Power Outage Hotline at 1-800-OUTAGES. Do NOT call your local utilities company. When the hotline receives confirmation of outages in an area, we will contact the appropriate channels.

Remain calm during outages. Most are caused by heavy weight or debris on power lines and will be fixed in a matter of hours. If an outage continues for longer than six hours, you are welcome to call the hotline for an update on the status of the problem. The hotline, unlike your local power company, is equipped to handle a large volume of calls. If you are placed on hold, please be patient, and someone will be with you promptly. This will free up power companies to focus their workers on fixing outages, not manning phone lines. Thank you.

22.

I have checked my phone 72,000 times. Still have service, still have battery, still no call from Dad.

It's been nearly twenty-four hours now since I texted him. Twenty-four long, excruciating hours. I'm sure of it this time, because I've checked compulsively and I've written it down.

Mom spent most of last night boarding up the door, so now I'm well and truly trapped.

At the moment, I'm pretty sure she's measuring water levels in our buckets again. God help me if anything's off. I haven't had a drop to drink without her permission, but she's not exactly behaving rationally. Could *she* have ingested blood? I can't imagine so. It's been so long since she's been out.

But we drank water filtered by our Brita for a while there at the beginning . . . They've said you'll show signs more quickly than that, but what the fuck do they know, honestly? Or what if . . . I glance down at the pinkish line on my palm, the mostly healed cut. I never showed it to my parents, and they never asked. Mom could have gotten cut on something, too, and never seen fit to tell me. She could have gotten blood in a scratch and thought since she felt fine at first, she'd pretend all was well.

Or this could just be how she's coping: an unsettling blend of obsessive-compulsive measuring and slow-growing religious fanaticism. I have to stop thinking about this.

With a sigh, I open my laptop to see if, by chance, anyone's online. But, of course, the Internet has decided to stop working. Dammit!

I slam my laptop shut, and with a collective, exhausted-sounding hum, everything goes black. Power outage.

For a few seconds, I sit stiffly in the darkness, blinking and blinking like that's going to magically give me night vision. My ears strain for sounds. There aren't many. A car sloshing down the street. A child crying in a nearby house. Nothing at all from *inside* the house. The hairs on my arms rise.

"Mom!" I shout. "Should I call that hotline?"

She appears in my doorway, her face a dancing shift of shadows in the light of the candle she holds.

"Don't bother. Other people will. I think we'll want to shut off our phones for now. Conserve battery."

"But I—okay." I can't very well tell her I'm hoping Dad will call. Not without explaining why.

I pretend to shut off my phone. I'll give Dad a couple more hours, at least.

"Come on," Mom says. "Help me set candles around the house."

I follow her into the dining area, where we've stored our entire stash of candles, just to be prepared.

We light several and set them out so that all the rooms are lit. It isn't nighttime yet, but without the candles, it is pitch-black in here. I wonder if, eventually, my body's clock will change. If one day, I'll go outdoors into the sun and find it so blinding, I'm forced back inside.

"Good thing it's not winter," Mom says cheerily.

Yeah, we won't freeze to death. I know that's a plus, but it's kind of hard to be cheerful about it, with everything else that's going on.

Mom busies herself in the bathroom. She's kept a bucket in there, just in case, for a time when we could no longer properly flush the toilet, since everything clogs so easily now and we don't want to waste our good drinking water. I decide to sit on the couch and not think about what she is going to do with it when the bucket gets full, now that we are all boarded up in here.

"What's that noise?" Mom calls from the bathroom.

I cock my head, listening. Oh shit, it's my phone. "Must've not turned my phone off right!" I shout back as I bolt for my room. "Sorry!"

It's Dad. I bang my shin against my chair as I fumble with my phone, and my *hello* is more like a groan of pain.

"Lea?" He sounds panicked. "Are you all right?"

"Yeah, fine. We just lost power. It's hard to see."

"I'm sorry I didn't call you back sooner. I'm still at the dam, as you might have guessed."

"Yeah," I say sourly.

"It's been a little crazy here. The gas got siphoned out of all our vehicles so no one could leave, and phone signals were rough for a bit there. But it worked out for the best. We're all set up now to see this thing through. You need to come. You and Mom. Get here as soon as you can, okay? It'll be safe."

"What do you mean, set up to see this thing through? Why didn't you at least *call* yesterday? I'm really—" I lower my voice. "I'm really worried about Mom."

"She'll be fine, if you get both of yourselves here. We have water, food, power, defenses. We're all set. Tell your mom I love her." Someone calls to him in the background. "I have to go, but I'll see you both soon, all right?"

"Okay, I'll tell her. We'll leave as soon as we can."

"Love you, sweetheart."

"Love you, too, Dad."

I hang up and rush into the bathroom, where Mom's still adjusting her bucket in the toilet bowl.

"Mom, we've got to go. That was Dad. He wants us to come to the dam."

"Oh, does he?" Her voice is as cool and sharp as an icicle.

"Yeah, he said they're all set up to see this through. And he says he loves you. He wants us to drive over as soon as we can. So . . . let's go."

"Honey." Mom takes my face in both of her hands. "We need to think about this. We can't just *go*."

"Why can't we?"

"Because." Her mouth thins. Actually, everything about her is a bit thinner. I hadn't noticed before, but standing here with her now, she looks older and sadder and more fragile than I've ever seen her. "I'm not sure it's possible to get there, in the current conditions. You need to let me think on it, okay? It's safe here, and I don't want to take you somewhere that might be less safe, on only your father's word. Now go turn off your phone. And then come back and show me that you've actually turned it off. I know you left it on purposely, before."

"Okay." I wither under her stern gaze.

My phone sits on my bed. I pick it up, touch the screen, look at its bright display. I can't just . . . turn it off.

I glance quickly over my shoulder. Mom's still busy with the toilet, humming what sounds like a church hymn under her breath.

Mom isn't sure about going there. I'll convince her. Have to turn my phone off now.

I send the text to Dad and glance over my shoulder again. She still hasn't come out of the bathroom. At least he'll know, even if I won't be able to get his response. Maybe he'll come get us. Or me, at least, if Mom refuses to come. I can only hope.

I wish I'd thought to ask him how long he's been gone. The way he talked, it didn't sound that long. I'm so sure I'm right, but I should have asked so I wouldn't have this small, gnawing termite of doubt.

"Lea," Mom calls. "Phone?"

If I'd been quicker, I could've texted my friends, told them to go to the dam, too. But Mom's feet are whispering over the carpet in the hall; it's too late now. I take a deep breath and press the power button on my phone until the screen goes black and it's just me and Mom and the darkness.

I sit stiffly beside Mom on the couch, a book in my hands. The flickering candlelight isn't ideal for reading. It's too low and uneven. But Mom is being weird and silent and was unreceptive when I suggested we play Monopoly or something. So I'm pretending to read because it's better than staring at the wall, which is what Mom's doing.

"If I go to bed," she says after a while, "can I trust you to leave your phone off, or will I need to take it?"

"You can trust me."

You so cannot trust me.

She narrows her eyes like she's read my thoughts. "Maybe I should take it, for tonight. Get it, please?"

"Seriously?"

"Yes. Now."

I sigh, disgruntled, and mope to my room. This sucks. I hold my phone, debating whether I have time to turn it on and check for a message from Dad. I don't think I do. A rattling sound echoes from the living room, then a banging. The front door. Dad!

I sprint back to the living room. "Mom, quick, we have to get the door open!"

"Quiet!" She whispers this, but it's such a foreboding whisper that I shut my mouth at once. "I don't think that's your father."

"Who else would it be?" I whisper back.

She presses a finger to her lips, and I'm silent. We creep closer to the front door. My heart thuds erratically.

"Use the crowbar," a voice says. Mom's right; this isn't Dad.

It's looters.

The door groans behind our boards. It's a pretty heavy door and has so many locks on it; hopefully it'll hold. Plus, there's all the plywood and boards Mom hammered over this side of it. But if they have the right tools . . .

Mom and I edge away again, into the hallway.

"What do we do?" I whisper.

"*You*," she says firmly, "wait here. I'll take care of it."

I want to protest, but I also don't want to go any closer to the door. What if the looters are armed?

"Be careful!" I hiss as she strides confidently back toward the door.

She stands just in front of it and shouts, "Back away from

the door! We're home and we're armed."

"We're armed, too," comes the reply. "And we're thirsty."

"We don't have enough water to risk losing your lives," Mom shouts back, which is a definite lie.

"We'll see."

Mom's nostrils flare. She rushes past me, back to her room, and comes out with a pistol. My chest catches. It isn't that I've never seen guns before. I have, plenty of times. In fact, my dad used to hunt when I was younger, and kept a couple rifles locked away here in the house.

But I didn't know Mom had this. It's shiny, new-looking. It's the sort of gun that's made only for one thing: shooting other people.

"Mom, what are you—"

"*Hush*, Lea," she snarls. "Go lock yourself into the spare room. Lock *all* the locks, and do not come out until I tell you it's safe."

Shaking, I do as she says. Twisting all the locks shut, I feel like I'm closing myself into a tomb. What am I supposed to do if she fails in keeping them out of the rest of the house? There aren't any weapons in here. I glance around. Buckets, gasoline canisters. A rocking chair. Some picture frames.

I'm the last line of defense for our water, but if they get in here, it'll mean they've gotten Mom, and how much of a chance do I have after that?

Bile rises into my throat, and I press my ear to the door. Mom's shouting something, but her voice is muffled. And then there's a crack, a gunshot. I jump back, tears pouring down my cheeks. I can't handle this at all. I don't want people coming to my home, trying to steal our things. This isn't fair, it isn't right.

I sink to the floor, covering my ears with my arms. I don't want to hear any more of it.

It feels like an agonizing amount of time passes before anything happens, though it may well have been less than a minute. Mom knocks on the door and says my name softly.

"Are they gone?" I ask, hovering near the door but not touching any of the locks.

"They're gone."

Still, I hesitate. She sounds very calm, confident. But they could be out there with her, holding her at gunpoint, forcing her to say those words.

"Honey, I promise." Her voice doesn't waver.

I have to trust her. She's my mom. So I twist open the locks and let her in. She's alone. I breathe a shaky sigh of relief, wiping slimy tears from my cheeks.

Mom envelops me in one of her pillowy hugs, and I cry into her shoulder.

"I didn't know you had a gun," I tell her.

"I know," she says.

I cry some more, because I can't seem to stop, no matter how many times Mom whispers that she will protect me, that I'm safe, that no one is going to hurt me *ever*.

You can't possibly make that promise, I want to tell her, but I don't, because maybe saying it is what makes her feel like she's surviving this, and it wouldn't be right if I took that away.

I wake in the night and know at once that I am not alone in my room.

I roll over groggily and look up at Mom, who stands over me with her hands clasped behind her back.

"What are you doing?" I ask.

"Just checking on you."

She pushes my hair away from my face. My skin crawls. But I remember how she reacted last time I flinched away from her, so I do my best not to move.

My mind flickers again to Dad, to his suggestion that we go to the dam.

"Have you decided about leaving?" I ask.

"Don't worry about that now. Just go back to sleep."

When she turns to leave, I swear I see a flash of silver in her hands.

I don't sleep the rest of the night.

I may never sleep again.

23.

In the morning, I wake to the smell of bacon. It turns my stomach, layered over the rotting animal stench of the blood. But I'm curious, so I roll out of bed and follow the glow of candles into the kitchen.

"Good morning!" Mom says cheerfully. In front of her, a breakfast feast sits on the island. Pancakes, bacon, hash browns.

"Thought I should use up some of the eggs and milk," she says in answer to my unasked question.

"Sure." I take the plate she hands me. "How did you . . ."

My eyes land on a propane grill beside Mom.

"Aren't those supposed to be outdoor only?"

"I was very careful," she says. I sense the subject is closed.

"Okay." I sit at the table with my breakfast. Mom just stands there and watches me eat. "Aren't you going to have any?"

"Of course." She mounds food onto a plate and sits beside me.

We eat in silence. I'm incredibly uncomfortable. I don't understand what's going on here, or why. "So about Dad," I say hesitantly.

She heaves a great sigh. "We have some things to take care of before we can think of leaving, sweetheart."

"Like what?"

She chews with her head tilted like she's deep in thought. "You know what we haven't done in a while? Looked at your baby pictures. Would you like to do that?"

"Um, sure. I guess. But—"

"Great!" She hops up, plate half-emptied, and then throws it in the trash. "You can do the same," she tells me. "We won't need our plates much longer."

I breathe a sigh of relief. If we're throwing out the plates, then she must not be planning to keep me here. We must be going to Dad soon. My heart accelerates and I shovel the rest of my pancake into my mouth. Mom has disappeared by the time I finish, so I dump my sticky, syrupy plate into the trash and search down the hall for her.

The basement door is open. Something thuds heavily along the stairs. Heart pounding even harder, I peer around the edge of the door, and then exhale roughly. It's just Mom, with a bloodstained storage container. My freaking baby pictures.

She hauls the thing to the top of the stairs, kicking off slippers that are soaked in red when she reaches the hallway.

"Mom, your legs," I say, pointing.

She looks down and lets out a very un-Mom giggle. The bottom several inches of her pajama pants cling to her legs, damp with blood from the basement. "I'll go change," she says, and leaves me standing there with the stupid storage container filled with crap I have no desire to look at.

The storage container weeps congealed blood. It slides slowly down the sides and settles on the floor, a sticky mess we'll never get clean.

It doesn't matter. We're going to Dad.

But what about after? We're throwing out plates and trashing the house. Do we plan on there not *being* an after? My throat tightens, and I back a couple steps away from the box. I don't want to look at these pictures. It might be closure for Mom, one last thing she does before we go, but it's not closure for me. I don't *want* closure. I want to believe that we're coming back one day, one day soon. I don't want the blood to destroy my entire universe so thoroughly and permanently.

But Mom reemerges cheerily from her room, in jeans now, and pries open the box. She hands me a stack of photo albums, grabs a bunch herself, and ushers me into the living room.

"You were such a happy child," she says. "Such a beautiful child. Remember when we went to Disney World?"

I feign interest in the six pages of pictures of the three of us there. I was six or seven at the time. "Vaguely."

"You were so excited to meet Snow White."

"Snow White? Really?" A fixation with Snow White is something I don't remember. A girl who gets poisoned by her stepmother and then revived by the kiss of a handsome prince doesn't really seem like my thing.

Mom smiles. "You thought she was very beautiful."

Oh, well *that* makes sense, at least.

"I always wanted your life to be more fairy tale than it's turned out to be," Mom says with a wistful sigh.

"My life's not over." I twist my hands in my lap. "Plus, fairy-tale lives are kind of overrated, don't you think? These princesses have to go through a lot of shit before their happy endings."

Mom blinks back tears. I pluck the photo album from her hands.

"I know it's hard to say good-bye," I tell her. "But this isn't a forever thing, right? We'll come home eventually. The important thing for now is to be safe."

She smiles tremblingly at me through her tears and strokes my hair. "You're right. It's hard to say good-bye, but being safe is . . . it's the important thing. It's the right thing."

"Of course." I nod emphatically. I'm not sure why this is taking so much coaxing. It's the only thing that makes sense. It isn't a long drive, and it's where Dad is.

"I love you." Mom kisses my hair. "I think I'm going to go do a few things in my room for now, if that's okay."

She leaves, and I stare down at the photo album. My smiling face, over and over. Wearing perfect little outfits my mom obviously chose for me, and wildly unmatched ones I obviously chose for myself.

Hillary and me, our hair in identical braids, riding our bikes in the school parking lot. Hillary and me again, a little older, looking utterly unimpressed that we had to stop whatever we were doing so we could be photographed. Our knees were too big for our bodies and our braces too big for our mouths, but we were kind of adorable.

I slam the album shut. I want to talk to Hillary, just for a minute. She's my best friend, and she has no idea if I'm even alive. Are her parents making her look at baby pictures, too? Have they boarded up their house? How is her brother doing? And their cat, even? I *have* to talk to her. It won't use that much of my phone's battery.

I sneak into my room. Mom's occupied; I don't see her, but I can hear her singing "On Eagles' Wings," a hymn I remember from one of the handful of times we've been to church in my life. I think the last time I heard it was at a funeral.

My phone sits on my bookshelf and I start to grab it, but

pause. One of my Bibles is missing. I haven't touched it in days. And I know I put it away.

Mom's singing louder. I do not care for this.

She's in the spare room, my Bible in her hands, rocking in a chair that once belonged to my grandmother. The tape measure she's been using to check our water supply sits at her feet. I can't believe she seriously checked *again*. She's been with me since the moment I woke. She knows exactly how much I've had, and how much she's had. What's to measure?

"Hey, Mom," I say, hooking my fingertips around the door frame. "What, um, what are you doing with my Bible?"

"Just reading," she says casually. "That's okay, isn't it? My King James was feeling a little too . . . Catholic."

She gestures to the floor, where the King James Bible she liberated from the basement weeks ago sits, disheveled. Mutilated, really. Some of its pages look torn. I don't know what she thinks she'll like better about the New International Version she holds now, but . . . what am I supposed to say? My whole life, she's been such an avid atheist. I never knew her parents very well, because she didn't want me "exposed to their falsehoods." And I've always been fine with that. Her childhood was different from mine. Scarier. She doesn't talk about it much, and once, when I was ten and started to have questions about why Gram and Gramp were so uptight, Dad sat me down and explained why I should never ask Mom about them, ever. About how when she was young, she was told she would go to Hell for tiny infractions if she didn't repent by stoically accepting harsh punishments, was brainwashed into believing the behaviors of most of her peers were sinful and wrong. How she lived in fear all the time, worried that even her *thoughts* weren't good enough for God. And how after she left for college, she never went back to her parents' house alone, for fear that they'd try to force her to stay. I can see why she gave up on God. And I can see why she wants him back. I have some questions about him myself that I'd love answered. But I don't like her methods, so I don't ask. Instead, I just say, "Oh. Yeah, that's fine. I'll . . . let you get back to it."

"Thank you."

I start to slip away, but before I can, she says, "Don't turn on your phone. I'll know."

Maybe mothers really *do* have extra eyes like they always claim.

"I won't."

Back in my room, I fiddle with my respirator. I should put it on. The window is starting to draw me again. I need to get over this. But I just want to see. See the beautiful ocean of red on my lawn, the lamb-white bones arching out of its depths.

Soon, I find myself thinking, like I'm talking to the blood. Soon we will leave here and we will drive through its depths. I don't know where this yearning has come from, this fondness. This *ache*.

I know it's wrong, and yet . . .

I press my face to the plywood.

"Lea? What are you doing?"

I jump guiltily. I didn't hear Mom come in.

"Nothing. Seeing if I could hear anything out there."

She doesn't believe me even a little bit, I can tell.

"Honey, are you . . . all right?"

"Of course I am. Why would you think I'm not?"

I say this knowing full well why she'd think I'm not. I was just thinking of the bones as *lamb white*. What the hell is that? I am so far from all right, it's not even funny. I should probably be taken to the hospital, because if this shit isn't delusions, I don't know what is.

"It's going to be okay," Mom says, and I'm not sure if she's talking to me or herself. "It will all be okay soon."

She starts humming "On Eagles' Wings" again, smiling at me beneath glossy eyes, and all I can think is that I am so not the only one in this house who's delusional.

24.

Covertly, I turn on my phone to send a text. I need outside communication. I don't just *want* it; I physically need it. It isn't the blood that's sucking rational behavior from my mind; it's isolation.

First, I check if Dad has texted. He hasn't, so I send a mass text to my most important people: Hillary, Aracely, Felix, Cadence. I tell them that if they need someplace safe, they should go to the dam. Then I send another text, to just Hillary this time:

My mom is freaking me out.

I don't expect any of them to reply. My phone keeps fluctuating between one and no bars of service.

But Hillary's response is almost immediate: W*ant us to come get you?*

I wish. Don't think she'd let me go.

Ur not going to the dam?

Eventually. I think. Not yet tho.

If ur in danger tell me ok?

Ok.

Am I? Mom hasn't actually done anything to me. She's clingier than usual, but can I blame her? Dad's gone. It's just us.

But she's getting really weird and intense and compulsive—there's no denying that. And Dad said we needed to go to him, but we haven't left. Why? Why not go and be safe?

I slip off my bed and peer out my doorway. Mom's in the spare room, counting and recounting our buckets of water. My Bible sits on the chair where she left it, a highlighter resting atop it. The King James Bible is nowhere to be seen.

"Mom," I say softly. "Can we . . . can we go? To Dad? Please?"

"Oh, honey." She comes to me, squeezes me too tightly. "We won't make it out there."

"We won't make it *here*. Not forever. Shouldn't we leave before things get even worse? It's only going to get harder."

"I know." She stares at me, like she's trying to imprint something onto my face. "It seems impossible, doesn't it?"

"Not impossible. Just hard."

"Honey, come here." She leads me to the living room. We perch on opposite sides of the couch. My whole body is tense. My heart beats in a weird, shallow way, like it's conserving itself in case there soon arises a moment where it needs to work extra hard. I should have told Hillary to come get me.

"You're not going to understand this," Mom starts, but a pounding on the door interrupts.

"Help us, please!" someone screams. It's not a voice I recognize. Not a voice I'd open the door for. "We're so thirsty."

I ball my hands into fists.

"As I was saying," Mom continues shakily. Her face is eerie in the flickering light of all our candles. "The world isn't like it was. This isn't going to get better. It's not going to stop."

"How can you know that?"

"Because—"

Glass shatters—one of our windows. Someone pounds on the boards Mom and Dad nailed over it. But they hold, for now.

"Because." Mom's voice is louder than before. "This isn't

a thing we can recover from. I don't think we're meant to."

"Says who? If you'd asked me a month ago, I'd have laughed in your face at the idea that the earth could start bleeding. We can't guess how it will turn out. We can't possibly know."

She smiles sadly. "Such an optimist. I had your optimism once. I thought my life held so many possibilities. I thought the bad things always got fixed. But they don't. Sometimes, they don't."

"But sometimes they do."

Another window breaks. I flinch.

Outside, a different voice shouts: "This house is barricaded. They must have water!"

"Mom, we have to go. Let's just give them the house. We'll take the car and go to Dad."

Another crash of glass, and our car alarm goes off. Fuck.

"*Mom.*" I grab her arm. "We have to do something."

"You're right. I'm sorry. You're right." She takes my face in both hands and kisses my forehead. "We need to do something."

More crashing glass, at the back of the house this time. Mom gets up and heads to the kitchen. I run to my room for my phone. I have to text Hillary one more time.

Don't come here. Everything's fine & I'll see you soon. xo.

I'm pretty sure everything's not fine, but it's too dangerous for her family to come here.

The boards on my window groan. Whatever's pounding on the other side shakes my whole room. I tuck my phone into my pocket, not sure what to do now. Mom said we had to do something, but she didn't say we were going to leave.

"Lea!" she calls. "It's time."

Time for what?

I grab my pocketknife off my desk. It's the only thing I have that could at all be used as a weapon. It disturbs me that I think I might need one.

Mom's standing in the living room with the car keys in her hand. A warning flares up inside me. But that might be thanks to the shriek of nail-against-wood from one of the bedroom windows. They're going to get in here. It's only a matter of time.

"Lea, come here." Mom beckons me closer. I obey, but cautiously. She holds tightly to my hand, and it's only now I see what I should have known she had: the gun.

"You think we're going to have to shoot our way out?"

I know why she really has it. I have known for days, in my heart. But I want her to say it.

"This gun . . ." Her voice is choked. Tears gloss her eyes. "This gun is going to keep us safe."

I lift my chin, stare her squarely in the eye. "How is it going to keep us safe? Say it. I want you to tell me exactly what you're going to do with that gun."

"I'm going to send us both to Heaven," she says, and it's so quiet I barely hear it over the sounds of people banging on all our windows.

"You don't even fucking *believe* in Heaven!" I scream. "I'm not ready to give up. You can't do this to me."

"You'll understand someday," she says. "Or you would, if . . . Lea, we're going to die quick or we're going to die slow. I love you and I will do *anything* to protect you. And that's why it's going to be quick."

The hell it is.

She starts to lift her arm, and I know she's going to shoot me, so I do the only thing I can and grab her by the wrist. We're screaming and fighting and slamming into the walls and the furniture, while people outside are slamming into our barricades. Mom trips and I go down with her, and the gun is still in her hand, but now it's my finger on the trigger, and if I could just get it free from her, we could get in our car and we could leave. We could be safe with Dad.

Except she's still fighting me so hard, even though I basically have her pinned to the floor, and then there's a blasting sound that echoes in my ears, my heart, my lungs, my very being. Everything goes silent—in here, outside. Everywhere.

Everything goes quiet because, as it turns out, it's incredibly easy to kill someone.

A gun will fire with just one little squeeze.

And now the bones in my hand hurt and Mom's got a hole through her throat and I'm a murderer. Or I will be when she stops gasping.

This isn't what I wanted. I didn't mean to do it.

I almost let the gun slip from my fingers, but she's still a little bit alive and I'm not letting her take me with her. I don't know how to find the safety on this damn thing or if there even is one, so I just sort of hold it away from myself, shaking.

Mom's staring at me with wide, sad eyes and breathing in horrible raspy pulls. She's suffering. I shot her, but I didn't do it right. The bullet went through at an angle. The perfect angle for this to be drawn out horrifically.

I don't want to shoot her again. I *can't* shoot her again.

"Mom," I whisper. "Mom, I'm sorry."

She shakes her head, something like a smile on her face, and I lean over her, pressing a hand to her cheek.

"I love you. I don't want you to die."

She mouths *I love you* back to me. I guess it's hard to speak when there's a bullet hole in your trachea. I did that. I put that hole in her throat.

"What can I do? I'll get some towels and—"

She grabs my wrist, the one with the gun. Grabs it with unexpected strength. She hasn't given up; she still means to kill me. Blood pumps out of the wound in her throat as she sits herself up, a wild, inhuman determination in her eyes, pushing the gun around toward me with both hands.

"No!" I scream. "You don't get to decide this for me, Mom. You *don't*."

I smash her in the face with my free elbow, and oh God, this is horrible. We're still both holding the gun, just like before, and this time maybe it'll be me who gets shot.

I wrap my finger around the trigger and fire it, over and over and over. Bullets slam into the wall, shatter a lamp, snuff out a candle, pierce the couch. I could have used this gun, this ammo, to protect myself later, but I have to discharge it to save myself now. Mom can't get it turned toward my face before it starts clicking, empty.

And then she gives up. She lets go of me, falling back to the floor, her throat and her shirt slick with fresh, hot blood. She's not rasping anymore, now she's choking. Her hands go to her neck, press over the wound like it will help her breathe. I want to be sick. I did this.

I stand up, back away from her, shove the empty gun into the side of my pants.

"I'm sorry, Mom," I tell her again. "I'm so sorry. But I want to survive this. I want to try."

And then, while my mother dies slowly on the floor, I leave.

25.

I leave with a crowbar, leveraging it against the boards in our door. The desperate scrambling outside ceased sometime during my fight, but I know they're still out there, waiting. Waiting to see what sort of person emerges.

I crawl through the opening I've made. Several people of various ages stand outside. They stare at me with fear on their faces. They're splattered with blood and carry all manner of blunt objects. They far outnumber me, and yet I frighten them.

"There's water inside," I say tiredly. "And gasoline. It's all yours."

I should have taken some of the water, maybe, but I can't bring myself to care. I walk down the steps and the group parts for me. I stop near the back of the group, when I see a familiar face.

Levi is here, holding hands with some girl I've seen but don't know. He must not care if I see, because he's had plenty of time to let go. I stare at their entwined fingers. Dirt-encrusted nails. Every line of their skin etched with blood. Slowly, my gaze drifts up, locks onto Levi's bright blue eyes, pronounced beneath the grime on his face.

"I didn't know you lived here" is all he says.

"I don't anymore."

And I walk away. I'm not even angry. He's just doing what everyone else is. He's just surviving.

Maybe he won't survive, or maybe he'll end up far, far from here, and I'll never have to tell Hillary I saw him. Thinking of her, there's a momentary flicker of something in my chest. Something small but feral and angry. I glance back at Levi, who's just walking through the door, his hand on the girl's back, guiding her. When he sees what's inside, I hope he remembers. For Hillary's sake, I just want him to disappear.

I haven't been outside in so long. I forgot my respirator, and it smells awful out here. Rancid. All the longing, the yearning, the aching I felt while trapped in my house fades like my mother's life did moments ago. The blood writhes around my feet, and I realize it's because our entire planet has become a perfect breeding ground for flies. Blood pools stagnantly on my lawn, and it's feeding thousands and thousands of maggots.

This should disgust me, but I feel nothing.

I walk slowly down my street, like I'm moving through a nightmare. I reach Cottage Street with its steep hill, and the rush of blood here seems less inviting to the flies, though it has caused the bones to tumble over one another, get tangled, and form little dams. It's oddly deserted, quiet—too quiet.

My eyes are drawn to Aracely's building, the bottom of which is drowning in the copper swells of the flooded river. Could she still be home? It's worth a shot. I'd rather make the journey to the dam with someone than alone.

The big, glass storefront windows on the first floor of her building are all shattered. So is the door that leads to the apartments upstairs. Main Street is wilder, less abandoned, than Cottage Street was. People scream and shout and smash things. It seems that while Mom kept me locked away, the rest of the world was stripped of civility, layer by layer, until all that was left was this primal, survival-of-the-fittest mess.

In the middle of the road, a man and a woman wrestle over a gallon jug of water. The man shoves the woman hard. She goes down with a great splash, disappearing beneath the blood.

She rises slowly, pushing herself up with her hands. Her face, her hair, her clothes, everything is slick with crimson. When she stands, gore drips slowly from her chin in gooey strands, and she stares down the man with eyes that look inhumanly white against her blood-soaked skin. It's like she went into the blood a human and came out a monster. Maybe she did.

And to me, suddenly, she is the embodiment of everything that's gone wrong here. And the embodiment of everything I need to become if I want to survive.

She lunges for the man once more, slamming his head against a parking meter. He falls, unconscious—or dead. The water is hers. Though her sanity is probably trapped somewhere in the nest of hair beneath the blood. Was it worth the exchange? I don't know. I'm not in a position to judge.

I turn away and haul myself up the soggy stairs, kick bones out of my way, knock on Aracely's door.

"Aracely, it's me," I say hoarsely.

She opens the door almost immediately. She's got a black eye and a split lip, and her apartment looks wrecked.

"What happened?" I press a finger gently to her lip.

"People broke in. Didn't believe me when I said we had nothing." She wraps a hand around my wrist and tugs me inside. "What happened to *you*?"

"I shot my mom," I whisper.

"You . . . you what?" Aracely pauses with the door still partly open.

"I didn't want to." I'm crying. The tears burn on my face. "I was just trying to get the gun away."

"She was, what, going to kill you?" Aracely has stepped back from me. "Your own mother? Lea, that doesn't sound right."

My knees give way, and I'm a puddle on the floor. "To save me."

"How would that save you? You're not making sense. Did you . . . did you get blood on you?"

I glare at her. "You mean *in* me? No. We've been alone in that house, and yeah, I'm not doing great but I'm not losing my mind. Not like she was. She said we'd die either way, so she was going to make it quick." My voice falls to a broken whisper. "I didn't have a choice. I just wanted to get the gun away. It was an accident."

"Christ." She kneels beside me. "I don't even know what to say."

"Where's your dad?"

"Gone. He went to get some more water and stuff yesterday morning. He hasn't been back. I guess he must be . . . I don't know. He's just stuck somewhere."

I'm lying on my back now, staring up at the whiteness of her ceiling. Something's missing from my heart, because suddenly it's like I've forgotten how to feel emotion at all. Maybe when you shoot a bullet through someone's neck, it takes a piece of your conscience with it.

"My dad said I should go to the dam. I wanted to go. My

mom, she just, she wouldn't."

"Is that where you're going now?"

I nod. "It's safe there, he said. I texted you about it. Did you get it?"

She shakes her head.

She's still kneeling beside me, her hair falling over one shoulder toward me in its long, perfect waves. I reach up a hand and slide my fingers through it.

"Will you come with me?"

"I don't . . . I'm not sure."

She has a look in her eye that feels familiar. It hides a wariness, a fear. Of me?

Of course, me. How could she not be afraid of me right now? I know how crazy everything I've said sounds.

"Please?" My plea is almost a whimper.

"Okay. Yeah. I'll go with you. It's safe there, you said?"

"Yeah. My dad told me they've got supplies and everything."

"Did you bring anything with you from your house?" she asks in a weird, forced-casual tone.

"Just my phone and my pocketknife. Oh, and the gun. It's empty, though."

"Can I . . . can I have the gun? The knife, too, just to see it?"

I know she doesn't really want to *just see it*; she wants me not to have a weapon. But maybe I shouldn't. So I hand her both. She takes them to the kitchen and puts them somewhere I can't see before crouching next to me again.

"Do we need to wait until your dad gets back before we go?" I ask.

She's silent.

"Aracely?"

"I told him right before he left. Told my dad. About you, about me."

"He took it badly?"

"Not . . . *not badly*. Just not . . . well." Her face is impassive, except a slight tremble around her mouth.

"You think . . . you think he didn't come back because he didn't *want* to come back?"

She shrugs.

"Aracely, your dad loves you."

Her face hardens. "And your mom loved you."

I cannot get enough air into my lungs. I curl into myself, dizzy and gasping. My hands find my throat. But it isn't my throat that's the problem, because I'm not the one with a hole there.

"I'm sorry." Aracely wraps her arms around me. "I shouldn't have said that. I don't think my dad left me on purpose. It's just the timing . . . But no, he didn't. He wouldn't. It's hard to find water right now, I know that. And, Lea, there was nothing you could have done differently, okay? I'm sorry."

"I could have not pulled the trigger." I sit up, wiping roughly at my face. She's wrong. There are *millions* of things I could have done differently.

"And then what?"

"And then . . . I don't know. God, Aracely, this is so fucked up. This is not a conversation two people should have to have. *Ever.*"

Her lips brush my forehead. I close my eyes and try to feel

something, but I'm empty.

"You took out your lip ring," she says, pressing a fingertip to my mouth.

"Yeah. It was uncomfortable with the respirator. It feels weird not to have it anymore, though. Like something's missing from my face."

"You can always get it redone, when—" She stops. There probably is no *when*; we both know that now.

My phone rings. Aracely and I both stare at it like it's a foreign object. Funny how something that's practically an extra limb for so long can become completely alien so quickly.

"It's my dad."

"Well, answer it!"

I do.

"Lea? Where are you? Are you and Mom on the way? Are you safe?"

"Mom is . . . she . . . I'm safe. But I'm not with Mom. And she's not . . . she's gone."

He's silent for a long moment, and I flash with anger. I told him I was scared and Mom wasn't okay, and he left me with her anyway. He just fucking left me.

"I killed her," I say in a cold, dead voice that doesn't sound like me at all.

"You . . . killed her." His voice is edged with disbelief, and something else. Something like fear.

"She was going to shoot me because she said it was the only way to be safe, and you weren't there so I had to save myself. I killed her so she couldn't kill me."

"Oh, Lea. Oh, honey. I don't know what to say." Fear,

definitely. "I never meant to abandon you, but your mom would never . . . she wouldn't ever . . . I don't know what happened, but there is no way your mother would try to kill you, sweetheart."

"She did," I say in that dead, icy voice again.

Silence follows, so long that I almost think he's hung up. Then, "Are you still planning on coming here?"

"Is it still safe?"

"Yes," he says softly.

"Then yes, I am."

"Okay. I guess . . . I guess I'll see you. Lea. Honey, are you sure you . . . are you sure about what happened to your mom? She told me about the day you saw blood on your floor, so maybe this—"

"This wasn't like that. Sorry. I wish it was."

He's desperate not to have heard what I told him, desperate to believe it isn't real. But it is and it's unfixable, and I can't stand listening to his hitched, borderline-sob breathing through the phone, so I hang up without another word.

"He doesn't trust me, I think," I tell Aracely. My core feels aflame. His distrust is burning me from the inside out. "Do *you* trust me?"

"Yes." She says it with a faltering smile and she takes my hand, but her palm is slick with sweat and I'm pretty sure she's lying.

The worst part of this whole thing is, I don't think I feel bad about what I did. There's a numbness in me; it starts in my chest and it's spreading out toward my limbs, like someone shot me through the heart with Novocain.

I don't deserve to go to the dam and be safe. I am a soul-less monster, and I belong in Hell. But I *am* going, because I killed my mother so I could live, and I won't give up on that now. Dad will believe me when I get there, when he sees how this has destroyed me. He will.

He has to.

26.

Aracely and I decide to stay here for the night. It's too late to try and get to the dam now, not with everyone out there attacking one another. We need daylight for some semblance of safety.

"The first thing we should do is get you into some different clothes," says Aracely. "We're close enough to the same size; some of mine should fit you."

While I wipe my blood-slicked hands and arms off with a towel, she rummages through her closet and finds me a pair of jeans and a T-shirt. I strip down to my underwear without shame. The jeans are just slightly too short, and just slightly too loose at the waist, but they'll do. The T-shirt fits me almost perfectly. I notice a few scrapes from my fight with Mom. I'll have to be careful not to get blood in them when we go back out.

The looters who attacked Aracely took every scrap of food in her house, and almost all the water. She has only one small bottle, which was hidden in a hole in her box spring. We split it, and it's wonderful, but it makes me hungry.

I'll be fine, though, until we get to the dam. A person can survive for weeks without food. I can make it one day.

Night falls and we both squeeze onto Aracely's twin-sized bed in an unspoken need to be nearby each other for a sense of safety, however false.

The roar of the river outside her window is fierce, so fierce that I actually can't hear any of the chaos going on elsewhere. Maybe I imagined it.

I wish I imagined it. All of it.

I blink and see a different future, one where none of this ever happened. Maybe Aracely tells her dad and her friends about us and we have the most perfect summer imaginable. Or maybe she doesn't. Maybe she keeps us a secret until the fall, when she stays with me under the guise of a UNH campus visit. It would be just us. Just her and me and my dorm room. Kissing until we can't breathe. Finding cheap beer and drinking it under the pretty trees from campus brochures. Taking the bus down to Boston so we can ogle the fish at the aquarium like huge nerds.

I blink again and it's gone. This is our only future now. The one where she and I curl together here on her bed and pretend we aren't terrified to go back outdoors tomorrow; the one where she pretends she's not afraid of me and I pretend I'm not afraid of myself.

I blink again, and there's blood running down the walls. Slow-moving fingers of it, undulating toward the headboard. I sit up, heart pounding, scramble to the foot of her bed.

"You okay?" Aracely mumbles sleepily.

I point to the wall. The blood is thickening: crimson curtains slowly closing behind Aracely's head. We can't escape it, no matter where we go.

Aracely's hand cups my cheek. "You look scared. What's wrong?"

"Blood," I whisper. "On the wall."

She turns. She sees nothing, I can tell. I'm imagining it again, just like in my room that day with Mom.

Mom.

"I'm sorry." My voice is thick and wavering. "There's nothing wrong except me."

Aracely gathers me in her arms. I cry into her shoulder, relieved she's not sending me away, terrified I'll look up at the wall and it'll still be bleeding.

"I'm here for you, okay?" She whispers it into my hair.

"Thank you."

I brave a glance at the wall. It's gone, the blood is gone. I crawl back across the bed and reach out to touch the white-painted surface with my fingertips.

It doesn't feel like anything. Just wall, smooth and cool. It was all a hallucination, just like before, and I'm not sane, just like before.

This isn't something I can think about right now. I need to believe that I'm still sane, because if I'm not . . .

If I'm not, that throws a whole bunch of things into question, and I really can't go there.

I pull my hand back and stare at my fingertips. Stained red. No, they're not. I squeeze my eyes shut and open them back up. Still red.

From beside my shoulder, Aracely lets out a startled cry. She grabs my wrist and holds my fingers near her face. "Where did that come from?" she asks.

I meet her gaze with a sharp twist of my head. "You see it, too? The blood on my fingertips?"

She lets my hand fall.

"I don't know where it came from," I tell her. "I touched the wall and then . . . it was there."

"We're tired," she says uncertainly. "It's been a really long, bad day and we both just need some sleep."

"That's probably it," I agree, because what's the point of arguing.

"It'll all be fine tomorrow, when we get out of here."

It'll all be fine, says everyone, ever since this started.

It gets harder to believe every time I hear it.

27.

We head out first thing in the morning. Neither of us has anything left except my cell phone, my pocketknife, and a couple steak knives from Aracely's kitchen. We don't even have respirators; mine's still on my bed at home and hers was stolen during the raid.

Maybe it's obvious that we've got nothing to steal, because even though there are still looters everywhere, no one bothers us much.

"We'll go to Hillary's," I tell Aracely confidently. "Her parents will help us get to the dam. They still have a car."

I try to text Hillary before we leave but it won't go through, even though my phone says I have service. I should have known it'd fail me sooner or later.

We slosh through the murk along the length of Main Street, past ruined businesses and smashed-out cars. It's *hard*. Painfully difficult. Breathing is challenging because of the air's thickness, and it seems the earth is truly, actively trying to destroy us now. Bones hide in piles, hook on to my toes. I rip my feet free of hair with every single step. Outside the historic inn, I have to lean up against one of its imposing columns and actually hack myself free with my tiny pocketknife, because hair tries to wind up my leg.

"This is going to be harder than I thought," Aracely says, her voice faint with exertion.

"We can do it, though," I say fiercely. "We have to."

Or else we'll die.

My unspoken words hang in the air as though painted there. Aracely nods, a firm, determined jerk of her head. And on we trudge, past building after building. We're getting there, slowly but surely. We pass the social security office and then it's just the church, a gas station, a few businesses, and we'll be on Hillary's road.

But I stop, suddenly, in front of the church, staring at those pink letters on its sign.

Beloveds, don't be afraid.

A horrible, shrill sob-laugh tears itself from my parched throat. I wonder who decided on that quote, one seemingly normal Sunday, and what has become of them now. Did they commit a murder-suicide? Open someone's throat for a bottle of water or a gallon of gas?

"We have to go inside," I tell Aracely. "Please, can we?"

I expect her to disagree, but she doesn't. She walks up the steps and tugs open the door.

Beloveds, don't be afraid.

I'm not afraid. And I'm fucking terrified. I don't know what I am anymore.

I walk past rows of wooden pews, scratched and marred and desperately in need of refinishing, and fall to my knees in front of a giant crucifix at the back. With my forehead pressed against Jesus's toes, I pray. I've never prayed in my life, and I have no idea what the fuck I'm doing, so mostly I just whisper *please* over and over and over again.

This church probably wouldn't let me set foot inside on a regular day, in our former world, and now I'm here, begging for a miracle at Jesus's feet. If the Bible is right, Jesus probably suffered even more than I'm suffering right now, and with that thought I feel so bone-achingly sad for him that I stand up and hug the cold, plaster Jesus, smearing blood from my clothes onto his emaciated abs. If Jesus did die for us, we were a wasted cause. He's probably dying all over again, watching the way we've turned on one another.

Maybe the blood had already done its damage before they told us to stop drinking water. Maybe it's diseased us all, irreparably. We're not zombies in the obvious way, where we're dying to feast on the flesh of our kind. But a different kind of zombie, where the blood has taken the part of our brain that cares about others and replaced it with this feral hunger for survival so strong, we'll do anything to appease it.

Or maybe this is just us. This is human beings, stripped of our pretenses. This is what we are at our cores.

Maybe the earth is right to destroy us.

"Lea."

Aracely's fingers are in my hair. I let go of Jesus, turn to her.

"We should go," she says.

"I know." I take her hand and she leads me back through the pews. But then I pause. "Would they have holy water here, do you think? We need water."

For a moment, she looks horrified. Then she gathers herself. "I'm not sure. We could . . . we could look, I guess. I don't see a font or anything up here, but maybe this church does it differently."

So we look. We take the stairs that lead to the church's basement, a falsely cheery place with long tables and a tiny kitchen. Blood has flooded it, several inches deep, but at least there don't appear to be any bones down here. Still, there's something sinister about all the religious posters and children's drawings taped to the walls above a sea of blood.

If there was ever holy water down here, there's not now. I think Aracely is equal parts relieved and disappointed. This isn't a Catholic church, but I still understand her hesitation, even if I don't share it.

"Okay." I look to her. "We can go now."

But when I turn back toward the stairs, I stop in my tracks. Someone's written on the wall there.

In blood.

I glance at Aracely again, not trusting my eyes. "You see that, right?"

She swallows hard. "Yes."

I step closer to the writing, touch my fingertips to the sticky red. The words raise goose bumps on my arms.

I will drench the land with your flowing blood
all the way to the mountains,
and the ravines will be filled with your flesh.
Ezekiel 32:6

"Have you ever read Ezekiel?" I ask Aracely.

"Yes," she says softly. "But it was years ago."

"And? Does it . . . end well?" I'm desperate for her to tell me yes. Yes, it ends well. It ends beautifully.

Her hands ball into fists and her shoulders tense. "I guess. I mean, the whole thing's pretty gruesome and awful, but it ends with . . . with hope. You don't—Lea, you don't really think this is like that, do you?"

I shrug. "I'd almost prefer it, you know? At least it's an explanation."

She looks away from me, failing to hide tear-glossed eyes.

I don't get it. I'm starting to understand why my mom turned back to religion. Science has failed to explain; we need something else, we need a *reason*. Everything's already gruesome and horrible. That part's a given. If it could end with hope . . .

I need the hope.

28.

It takes us over an hour to reach Hillary's after leaving the church, but finally, thankfully, we do arrive.

"Hillary!" I call out, and pound on her door. It flies open beneath my fist.

Shit.

It smells like death inside. Or maybe it smells like nothing, and I'm just paranoid. But it's quiet, so quiet. Too quiet. I resist the urge to take off my shoes and leave them on the mat. Hillary's mom won't care about shoes. Not now.

In the living room, I find Hillary's dad. I can't tell how it happened, but he's very clearly dead. There's a smaller—much smaller—form half underneath him.

My stomach squeezes itself up into my throat. I turn away. I absolutely cannot think about that smaller form. About the fact that Hillary's dad must've died trying to protect Finn, and failed.

I feel like someone's wrapped my brain in gauze. Like I am filled with this sickening fear-sadness-horror, but the gauze is holding it in so I'm aware of its existence without actually *feeling* anything. But my hands shake as I go through the archway into the kitchen. All the cupboards are open, food and water gone, but it's empty. So is the dining room.

But not the laundry room.

Hillary's there, on the floor, her face bashed into an unrecognizable mash of caved skull and broken flesh. Her mother's body lays next to her. Most of it. Whoever killed her hacked chunks of flesh and entire limbs right off her.

I freeze in the doorway, Aracely at my back. My mouth is

open, but all that comes out is a strangled whimper.

Who would do this to someone? Who *could*? This is so violent and messy, something beyond desperation for food and water. This was done by someone who lost their sanity altogether. Or else this is some kind of nightmare. Please let it be a nightmare. *Please.*

I dig my nails into my arm. It hurts. A lot. And Hillary's still there. Dead.

I can't be in this room anymore. Cannot see my best friend's corpse. Cannot let this image become any more permanently emblazoned on my brain.

I back away quickly, bumping into Aracely. I run to the back door of the house, throw it open, flee to the forest behind Hillary's yard. Where I fall to all fours, splattering bile into the blood that pools here.

Maybe Hillary's the lucky one. Hillary died quickly. There might have been pain, but it can't have lasted long.

I'm going to die, too. Everyone's dying. Only, when I die, I'll die as a person who has killed her own mother. Not a person who died with their loved ones.

Maybe Mom was right. Maybe she *was* protecting me when she tried to kill me. If she'd succeeded, I wouldn't have become a murderer. Wouldn't have walked past Levi and that girl and all those other people who probably would have hurt me themselves if I hadn't freely given them our supplies. That was my second chance; Mom failed, but if they hadn't all been so terrified of me, and I hadn't been so indifferent, I could have died then, at the hands of desperate, thirsty people. I wouldn't have seen my best friend and her whole family, dead. I wouldn't be out here in the woods with blood swirling down the hill past my knees while I vomit up my guts. What part of this did I think was preferable to death? What fucking part?

My fingers find something in the ground. Something rough and rusty feeling. There's all kinds of crap back here; I know that from years of slicing myself on junk and of my mother bringing me to the doctor for my millionth tetanus shot. I pull the rusty thing free. It's a lawn mower blade. Bent and ancient, but still very, very sharp on its edge. It feels like my death was meant to be. Like this was put here so I could slit my throat and be done with it. It's going to happen eventually, regardless. Isn't that what the quote meant, in the church? I may as well end things now before my suffering worsens. Before I hurt anyone else. If there is a God, I can only hope he's as merciful as they say.

"Lea."

I turn my head. Aracely's right behind me.

"I know what you're thinking," she says. "And don't you dare."

I pull myself to my feet, holding tight to the blade.

"We're going to die anyway." My voice is a harsh scratch. "What's the point of keeping on like this? What's the point of drawing it out?"

"That's not true. It's nowhere *near* an inevitability that we will die. You have fought so hard not to die."

Tears are thick on my cheeks. When I think about the future, I only see death. It's happening right now on the streets: people murdering each other for food and water and God knows what else. Everyone's so desperate for survival, and so unlikely to succeed. I don't want to be part of it anymore. Survival is just not worth it.

"And what will be left if we live?" I whisper.

Aracely's face hardens. "Nothing, I guess. Nothing at all. No, you're right. Killing yourself is the only way out."

She pushes against me, twists my arm so that the mower blade is pressed right up to my jugular.

"Aracely, stop it. Don't make yourself part of this."

"I'm not." She presses it a little harder, so that I can feel its roughness against my skin. "I'm just making it easier for you. It's right there; all you have to do is push."

I could. She's right; it's so easy now. My vein throbs beneath the pressure.

A sob rips from my throat. I could die. All I have to do is commit. It could be over with one little slice. I could be free of this horror, just like Mom wanted. Grant her dying wish.

Do I want that?

I shove against Aracely, and she steps back. The blade splashes to the ground. I sink onto a nearby rock, hugging my knees, a mess of ugly tears and gasping sobs.

Aracely kneels in front of me. "I'm sorry," she says. "I shouldn't have."

"I needed it." I press my face into my knees. "I don't want to die. I just . . . I don't want to live, either. Not like this."

I reach for her hand. She dodges my grasp and closes her arms tightly around me instead.

"We have to keep going now," she says, her breath warming my neck. "When we get to the dam, it will be better, I know it will."

"Yeah." I hug her tighter. We should get up, get away from this death-filled place. But my body is trembling with shock and fear and relief, so for the moment, I'm frozen here.

"My best friend is dead," I say.

"I know." She slides her fingers through my hair. "I saw."

We stand like that, locked in a desperate embrace, in a silence broken only by the raggedness of our fearful breaths.

"My dad could be dead," Aracely whispers, after a bit, like it's only just occurred to her.

So could mine, I think, but I don't say it aloud. I can't plant doubt in the soil meant to grow our only hope.

"All my friends . . . fuck, Lea, they could all be . . ."

She steps away from me, rubbing her eyes hard with her palms. "I'm so sorry, I shouldn't be doing this now, but it's just, I never thought . . . I thought they'd all be okay, and now I don't know."

I can't escape the image of what I saw inside Hillary's house. It's in my memory forever, and thank *God* none of Aracely's friends live on our route, because I don't want her to experience anything like that. I don't want *anyone* to, ever. I feel myself breaking a little bit more. Hillary is gone, *gone*. Her family, my mom, I can't deal with this, I can't deal with more.

"Please don't die," I say. "I need you."

She kisses me. It's probably disgusting, with my vomit breath and tears slicking my whole face. "I'm going to do everything I can not to." A pause. "You?"

"As long as I still have you."

I know how desperately clingy that sounds. How Romeo and Juliet idiotic. But I don't care, because at this point, Aracely is all that anchors me here. The world is chaos. Everyone I know is dead or dying.

But I still have Aracely, who shines like a star, like the moon, like the sun. She is hope, personified. It's dangerous to tie so much onto a single person, onto this girl I've been dating for mere weeks, but it's all I have. *She's* all I have.

It was only minutes ago that I wanted everything to end, but I'm so thankful she stopped me. I *have* fought hard to survive. I'll continue fighting.

"Aracely." I kiss her, a hard and hungry kiss. "We're going to do this together, right? We're going to make it."

"Yes," she says, and I don't care if it's a lie. "We're going to do this together, and we're going to make it. This fucking planet will not take us down. We are too young. We have so much left to do."

I fish around in the blood near my feet until I find the lawn mower blade again. Aracely's eyes widen with concern when I pull it out.

"No, it's not—I just think we're going to need more weapons."

She smiles at me. Moves to get up. The smile slides off her face.

"The hair," she says. "The fucking hair is holding on to my feet."

I jump off the rock and hack at the strands around her legs with my blade. It tears, and tears some more, until finally she's free. But I feel the hair grasping at my ankles now, too. I jump back onto the rock, and pull her up with me. We stand there, clinging to each other, like we're on a tiny island.

"It's getting worse," she says.

"Yeah. This is not going to be easy."

But now I'm angry. I mean seriously: fuck this planet. It

is doing everything it can to destroy us, and I'm not letting it have me. I may end up dying. If I'm honest, there's a pretty big part of me that still thinks death would be a relief. But I'm not going to die because the earth pinned me down and drowned me, or because blood slid down my throat and I lost what's left of my mind. I will get to the dam, I will get to my dad. I'm going to try my absolute hardest to survive this, just to spite our goddamn planet.

And it starts right now.

29.

At a car dealership just up the road from Hillary's, we find an older model F-350 with big, heavy tires and a lift kit.

And we steal it.

It's unlocked, but the keys aren't inside, so Aracely hot-wires it. There's a tool chest in the truck bed, and she uses a couple of screwdrivers to pry open the panel beneath the steering column. Here, she pauses, glancing at me from her position on the truck's floor.

"Don't judge me," she says.

"I'm not."

Actually, watching her successfully start a vehicle by twisting wires together or whatever else she's doing under there, I'm proud of her. Proud and impressed. And I kind of want to kiss her.

So when she finishes wrapping everything in electrical tape and jumps to the ground, I do kiss her. Because it feels like any moment could be the last moment, and I want all the moments to be perfect. She leans into me and hooks her thumbs into the waist of my pants, holding me against her for a few peaceful moments before we get into the truck.

"I've always wanted to drive something like this," I say, adjusting the steering wheel so I can actually see over it. Thank God my dad taught me how to drive a standard. My foot can barely compress the clutch far enough, but that's fine. We've got so much clearance and the truck has a half tank of gas, which is more than plenty to get us to the dam. It also smells like hay (probably from the baling twine in the backseat), and hay is one of my favorite smells in the world.

It's a significant improvement over the rancid stench of rotting blood.

Slowly, I steer us out onto the road. We grind over bones, slosh through blood. It seems to be going okay, though.

Until I reach the interstate.

There's a man standing in the middle of the on-ramp. With a rifle.

"Run him over," Aracely says calmly, gripping the dash. "Just run him the fuck over."

I know that's what I should do. I have every intention of turning this threatening man into roadkill, but my foot goes for the brake instead. He has that gun, and I know now how easily desperate people can become killers. What does he have to lose if he knows he's about to die?

The truck splutters and stalls. Shit, I forgot I was driving a standard. There's a burst of noise, and the windshield explodes into a powdery rain of glass. I close my eyes and throw up my hands.

The truck door opens and the man tosses me roughly out. I land on the ground in a splash of blood. Something sharp catches me in the ribs and the breath leaves my lungs. But I keep my face above the surface—that's the important thing.

The man screams at Aracely to get out of the truck, and I pray for her to listen. He could kill her with that rifle. Kill her so quickly.

She listens. I hear the slam of the passenger door, and then she's beside me.

"Can you get up?" she asks gently. I think she's mad, though. Her voice has a hard undercurrent.

I start to stand, but then the barrel of the rifle is pointed directly between my eyes and it is all I can do not to piss my pants.

"Keys!" he demands.

"We don't have any."

"So the truck started by what—magic?" he sneers.

"Someone hotwired it for us," says Aracely.

"One of you. It had to be. Do it now."

Neither of us moves. He presses the gun to my face. I breathe out, long and slow. It'll be fitting when he kills me. Karmic justice probably. I close my eyes. It's better if I just accept it.

"I'll do it," Aracely says. "Hang on."

The gun doesn't move, but I hear Aracely sloshing through blood. I open my eyes. She's on her back beneath the steering column, just like before. My heart races.

And then, in the space of a blink, she's out of the truck, slamming the steering column's panel into the man's side. It knocks him—and the gun—onto the ground, away from me.

By the time I get to my feet, Aracely has a piece of baling twine wrapped around his throat. With one foot on his back, she yanks hard on her end of the twine, tightening and tightening.

He's suffocating.

He's drowning.

He spits burbling gasps from beneath the blood. It sounds just like my mom's breathing did, at the end.

I don't know exactly which way he dies, but die he does.

Aracely lets go of the twine and turns to me, panting with exertion.

"You okay?" she asks.

"I think. You?"

She nods.

"I'm sorry." I wrap my blood-soaked arms around myself. "I shouldn't have hit the brakes. But the gun . . . I just . . ."

She doesn't say anything. I think about how quickly she turned into a killer, and I'm a little frightened of her. Is this how she felt about me? Still feels, maybe?

She should, because I did the same thing. I can still feel the smoothness of the trigger against my finger, the vibration as the bullet left the pistol. It's part of me now, all of it, the entire horrific sequence of events.

Aracely tries to restart the truck, for real this time, but the engine whines and won't catch. She frowns and pops the hood. Which she stares into, frowning even harder.

"What's wrong?" I ask.

"Come see."

I know nothing about vehicles and how they work, but I don't need to. The problem here is evident. Hair has wound itself around most everything under the hood. It crawls like snakes, threading and tightening, and there's no way we're getting this truck started now.

"I'm sorry," I say again.

"It's fine," she snaps, her hands tightening on the edges of the truck's hood.

"But—"

"I suspect," Aracely interrupts in a tired, emotionless voice, "that this would have happened regardless. Like what happened with Hillary's car that day."

I shut up, because her mentioning Hillary's name right now feels like a punch to my lungs, and because the way she's glaring at me makes me want to crawl beneath the blood and let it fill my lungs until I no longer exist.

"We should maybe take some of the baling twine and stuff," says Aracely, turning away like I don't even exist. "And then . . . and then get walking, I guess."

I go to pull myself up into the truck, but end up doubled-over, clinging to the bottom of the steering wheel, when a searing pain flashes in my side.

Aracely doesn't notice until she's clambered in from the other side and sees me slumped half on the floor.

"Lea? You okay?" She picks carefully across the glass-littered bench seat and jumps down beside me.

"I don't know." I straighten, grimacing. "Something hurts."

I lift my shirt partway. A rib is sticking out of my skin. I nearly faint before realizing that the bone doesn't belong to me. It's small and broken and lodged into my flesh right between two of my own ribs. This explains the pain in my side when I fell.

Aracely removes the bone. It comes free with a gross popping sound and a trickle of blood.

"Thanks." I sit on the truck's runner, a little dizzy. Not from the wound or the sight of blood, just everything catching up to me, I guess.

"We should really clean that up." Aracely's eyebrows pull together concernedly. She touches my side with her finger-tips, and it doesn't even make me feel anything. "There were some rags in the tool chest."

She hops up into the bed of the truck and pulls out a whole stack of grease-stained rags.

"Not the cleanest," she says, "but better than the alternative."

Gently, she wipes my wound clean, then each of us takes another rag to wipe what we can of the blood off our skin, because we probably have a million micro-scratches from the spray of glass when the windshield shattered.

"I wish we had an antiseptic or something for you," she says, frowning.

"It's not that deep. It'll be fine."

I can tell she disagrees, but she doesn't contradict me. Instead, she hands me the dead man's rifle and hops back into the truck for the baling twine and whatever else might be in there.

The rifle feels wrong in my hands. Worse than the pistol. It's long and sleek, meant to kill much larger animals than humans. But it is the only protection we have.

"Ready?" Aracely asks, shoving the baling twine deep into her pocket. I watch her do it, and try not to relive what just happened. She killed that man like it was nothing.

"I'm ready," I say.

It's going to be a long and tedious walk, but we've still got at least half the day. We'll be fine.

As we slog through the blood, I concoct a horrible backstory about that man, in my head. Maybe *he* was the one who murdered Hillary and her family. If he was, he certainly deserved to be killed.

Anyone who tries to murder someone deserves it when they're killed.

Don't they?

"Aracely, do you believe in an eye for an eye?" I ask.

"Um. I don't know. Why?"

I shrug. "Just wondering. I mean, if someone does something really horrible or tries to, then they deserve it if you do something horrible to them in return. Don't they?"

Her mouth twitches downward. "It depends."

"On?"

"Whether or not they had a choice."

We fight the blood up a steep incline. I still cannot understand how it can be constantly flowing downward and yet there's always more. I try not to think about the church and the quote about valleys filling with blood. Is that really how we'll end?

When we reach the top of the hill, we run into a family desperately pushing their minivan.

"Hey!" The mother comes at us, and I tighten my hands on the rifle. "Do you have phones?"

"I don't, sorry," says Aracely.

I reach into my pocket, but nothing's there. I had mine when we left Aracely's, but I suppose it could have fallen out anywhere. "Me neither."

The whole family has stopped their futile efforts at moving the car and are staring at us now. The husband comes over and places his hands on the wife's shoulders. He eyes my gun.

"Where did you get that? Girls your age shouldn't have guns like that."

"Why shouldn't we?" Aracely's eyes narrow. "People our age can get hunting licenses and use rifles. Even *girls*." She emphasizes the word *girls* with a sweep of her hair and a snarl in her tone.

"So you know how to use that rifle safely, then? Either of you?"

"Yes," I say defiantly. I took hunter safety a couple years ago, with Hillary and Felix. The fact that I've never actually shot an animal is irrelevant.

You've shot a person, my mind whispers.

I had to. I had to, I had to.

"You shouldn't be out here like this," the woman says. "It isn't safe. Let us help you."

She takes a step closer and I snap.

"Back off!" I shout, aiming the gun at her. My finger slides so smoothly into place on the trigger. "Back the fuck off, or I swear to God I will shoot you."

She stumbles back, all the way to the van. She and her husband cover their three small children with their bodies, and I lower the gun immediately. I wouldn't have—I could never have shot children. Never.

"Just leave us alone, okay? Just let us be." My voice breaks, and I turn away from them.

"We need to get off the road," Aracely whispers to me. "If there are others like that, we might be in for trouble."

"You're right. And . . . take this. Please." I shove the gun at her. She doesn't protest.

We abandon the road in favor of the forest that borders it, giving a wide berth to what used to be a swampy area. I saw a moose there once, when I was a kid. No danger from moose now, but who knows what this blood would do to land that was mush to begin with. Probably it would pull us under before we knew what had even happened.

I trip and fall hard, over a bone or a root or a branch—

it's impossible to tell. Aracely helps me up without a word, handing me another of our rags to wipe my skin clean. Every step is a struggle. A war against the earth. Webs of hair, underlayers of debris, it all seems to be actively trying to impede our progress.

And the blood is rising. Slowly, but it is rising.

I will drench the land with your flowing blood all the way to the mountains.

It's stuck in my head, that quote. Like when I read it, it peeled itself off the wall of the church basement and glued itself onto my brain. Because as far as I can tell, it's prophetic.

"I think this is going to be a problem," Aracely says after a while. "The blood."

"Yeah, let's get off the ground."

We find a tree, a big old maple with lots of thick, sturdy branches, and we climb it. Not a moment too soon. The blood starts bubbling ferociously. It froths and sloshes as it rises higher and higher. I'm pretty sure it's at least waist level when it slows, and I clutch my tree branch tightly, thankful for its height.

"Aracely," I say softly, a very horrible thought settling over me. "I'm not sure we'll make it there tonight."

She lets out a long, long sigh. "I'm not sure we will, either."

So close, and yet so far. A twenty-minute drive turned into a multiday nightmare. I slump against the tree trunk, closing my eyes against the disappointment.

The blood keeps rising. It drives us higher into the tree, as high as we can go without risk of falling. My knees and feet and back ache from crouching, but aside from shifting position every now and then, we really can't move. Some-time during the night, the blood stops rising, but it's high—several feet, definitely—and it doesn't go back down.

It froths and sloshes, belching debris from its depths and then gulping them back down.

"What if—" I start, but Aracely presses her fingertips to my mouth.

"Don't," she says. "I can't, just don't."

I nod and adjust my position, leaning against the trunk, dangling my legs on either side of a thick branch. I watch the mess of crimson below, and it feels like I'm waiting to die. My throat is tight with thirst, my stomach closing over itself with hunger. I run my nails over the bark of the tree, rough and gnarled and tough. I don't think maple bark is edible and the night temperatures are too warm for sap, but maybe if I drill a hole with my knife, *something* will happen? I try it, hacking at the bark.

"What're you doing?" Aracely asks.

"I'm trying to get some sap out or something. I don't know. I just need something to do."

"Okay."

She doesn't say much else to me for hours. And that's how long I'm digging at the bark: hours. My fingers are cramped from holding tight to my tiny pocketknife, but I've nothing to do except this. Aracely's still angry with me for hitting the brakes when we were in the truck. Every time I try to strike up conversation, she answers as succinctly as possible and goes back to staring at nothing. And when I flat out ask her if she's mad, she snaps, "What do you think, Lea?" We don't speak again for a long while after that.

Without her to talk to, I need a task to keep my mind from wandering. To Mom. And Dad. The blood-scrawled quote. Hillary's broken corpse, and Finn's. Aracely's hands around that twine, the man's choking gasps of death. That family before, pushing their van. Three young children, and the blood, so high now . . .

I dig more roughly at the tree. I've gotten past the outer bark, and now I'm scraping and rotating, trying to make a hole that's at least somewhat circular. I stop when the hole is as deep as my knife can make it. My back aches, badly. I stretch, roll my shoulders, and Aracely says her first word in what feels like half the night: "Careful."

"I know." It comes out more sullenly than I meant. I desperately want her to stop being angry with me, and acting like a jerk won't help. "Thanks."

She smiles thinly. I think she wants to stop being angry, too. "So? Find any sap?"

I stick my pinkie finger into the hole I made. Nothing. I shake my head. "Sorry."

"It's okay. The season's wrong, isn't it?"

"Yeah."

I readjust my position again. I'm so exhausted, but I can't sleep or I might fall. And if I fall, I will die. The blood will tear the flesh from my bones, and it'll fill the ravines with all the rest. But I'll be at peace. I'll be with my mom. I'll—

Jesus *Christ* what is wrong with me? I shake myself to clear my head.

"Everything okay?" Aracely asks. Her voice is tight, and I wonder if she's having the same struggle as me.

"Yeah. Just trying to get comfortable . . . ish."

That *is* what I'm doing. She doesn't have to know what's going on in my head.

I spend the rest of the night, the entirety of the next morning, and most of the afternoon in the most uncomfortable position I can without it being painful. I hardly move at all. My whole body aches, and my brain is fuzzy with exhaustion and hunger and thirst, but I'm alive and I'm safe and that's what matters. At one point midmorning, Aracely starts to nod off and I grab her arm, terrified.

She jerks awake with a shriek, clinging to both my arm and the branch she's sitting on until her breathing has calmed. Then she shifts, making herself more uncomfortable, like me.

In the early afternoon, the blood starts to recede. And by late afternoon, it seems to have reached a point where it intends to stop. Lower than it's been since the early days.

"Do you think it could be . . ." I trail off because I don't want to jinx it with the word *ending*. But that's what this feels like, to me. I don't know how things go in Ezekiel, but the floodwaters eventually disappeared in the story of Noah, didn't they? I don't know why I'm clinging to Biblical explanations, but they're all I've got right now. All that's giving me hope.

"It could be," Aracely says. "Let's go find out."

30.

We spend the night in a hunting camp we find nearby, because it's too late and the moon too new for us to attempt to continue toward the dam tonight. Calling it a hunting *camp* might be an overstatement. It's a wooden platform with wide-gapped walls on three sides. There's a loft tucked up under the roof at the back. It's maybe four feet wide and is reachable only by a rope ladder that we have to pull down with a tree branch. But judging by the blood-soaked walls of the structure, the loft is high enough to keep us safe if the blood rises again. To our delight, there's a tiny cooler in the corner, and it has a couple packages of beef jerky in it. The kind you buy from a store, with a million preservatives and an expiration date years away.

We're both ravenous, so we eat it all, but then I sort of wish we hadn't because it's salty as hell and now I feel like someone's taken a sponge and absorbed all the remaining water right out of me. Thirst is a much bigger problem than hunger, and it's been at least forty-eight hours now since either of us had a drop to drink. This is bad.

"How's your side feel?" Aracely asks. She's leaning against the wall, one leg stretched out and one arm resting on her other leg. In her perfectly fitting, blood-spattered jeans and olive green tank top, she looks like a badass character from a video game. I don't know how she does it. I'm pretty sure I just look gross.

"It feels all right." Actually, it feels achy and gritty, but there's no reason to tell her that. It's not like she could help. Besides, *all* of me feels achy and gritty.

"That's good," she says. And that's all she says. She's clearly still angry with me about yesterday, but what was I supposed to do? It's not like I've been trained for a scenario like this. The silence stretches on painfully. So painfully, I swear it's manifesting physically in all my cuts and scrapes and bruises. I don't want a repeat of the past twenty-four hours, which was mostly silence and resentment and misery.

"What do I do to make you stop being mad at me?" I ask, and I sound pathetic.

Her face softens. Her whole body softens. "I'm not *mad* at you," she says. "I mean, I was, but I'm trying not to be. I'm just . . . You killed someone, Lea, and I don't know what to do with that. And I killed someone, too, and I don't know what to do with that, either."

"Neither do I."

"It scares me."

"Do *I* scare you?"

She hesitates before answering. "A little, I guess. Yeah."

"You scare me a little bit, too." I hug my knees. "So is it good or bad that we both scare each other now?"

"I don't know." She smiles, ever so slightly. "Both, maybe?"

"I feel like a hypocrite. I shot—" My voice catches and I have to clear my throat before I can go on. "I shot my own mother, and you, you were just saving my life."

Aracely reaches out a hand. I take it. Just the ends of our fingers are hooked, but still, it soothes me.

"You were saving your own life," she says quietly. Then, "Maybe it's not each other we're afraid of. Maybe it's just all of this. These things we've had to do and see, they're not things we should have to have done or seen. Maybe that's what we're really scared of."

"Maybe. Probably." I smile at her, though a smile isn't the right expression for how I feel. I have this bone-deep sorrow, and I don't know what could ever make it go away. I miss my mom and I want her back.

"I shouldn't be scared of you anyway," Aracely says, her voice falsely light. "I'm pretty sure I could take you."

I laugh, and it surprises me. It's a real laugh, not like the harsh, depressed imitations I've managed recently. And it feels really good. "You could not! I'm stronger than I look."

"Are you?" She grins and leans forward, squeezing my upper arm. "Your arms are sticks compared to mine. I have hideous man arms."

"You have perfect arms."

She kisses me. Pushes me back gently and pins me to the floor of the loft.

"Told you I was stronger," she whispers into my ear, then kisses the side of my jaw.

"I'm pretty sure it's cheating if you use kissing as a weapon."

She laughs, and it vibrates against my skin. Her fingertips trail down my arms, and we're kissing again, and this is so much better than talking about the people we've murdered.

We need this, I think. Both of us do. This moment of normalcy and reconnection among all the death and the horror. We're not going anywhere—at least not tonight—and there's no one around to stop us, either.

So we don't kiss like people who are trying to cram all the kissing they can into a few precious moments like we have before. We kiss slowly, delicately, achingly. Brushes of skin and fingertips and mouths.

When she reaches for the button on my pants, my impulse is to stop her, tell her it's not really the right time for that, but I remember how I wanted all my moments to matter, and I just kiss her harder and let it happen.

And then I'm lost, and there are no thoughts in my head at all except how blissful I am in this moment, which I will cherish forever.

No matter how long or short that forever may be.

31.

I wake in the night to the sound of Aracely crying softly beside me. I turn my head toward the shadow of her form. She's hugging the rifle. Hugging it tight, like she doesn't intend to give it up for anything. When I look at the shadowed lines of her face, I see guilt.

And I run.

I didn't survive my mother just to be murdered by my girlfriend.

And I certainly don't want to have to kill someone I care about for my survival again.

I jump down from the loft, my bare feet splashing into the warm, thick blood. The mat of hair tangles around my toes, but I run out of the hunting camp and into the night as fast as I can.

Aracely's calling after me. I move away from the sound. A root trips me and I go down, hard enough that I need a pause to catch my breath.

I'm dizzy when I stumble back to my feet. The shadows swirl around me. I have to lean against a tree with my eyes closed to steady myself. We really should have made water a priority. No, it's not *we* anymore. I. *I* should have.

"Lea, would you get the fuck back here?" Aracely shouts. "I wasn't going to shoot you."

Wasn't she? Maybe I misread her. But maybe I didn't. What if I didn't, and I go back, and she kills me?

I crouch down. I'm so covered in blood, it doesn't matter anymore. It's probably already seeping into all my cuts and scratches, infecting my brain with its toxins. Aracely still calls to me, and now I creep cautiously toward the sound of her voice. If only it weren't so dark. I can't see her or anything else.

She stops shouting to me, and I stop moving. The slice in my side stings, and I've got a dizzy pressure in my head.

What's she doing? Trying to find me? Giving up? What?

"Lea."

She's beside me. I scream.

"I didn't even bring it out of the camp." She grabs my arm tight. "I don't have the gun with me right now."

She's close enough that I can see her faintly through the dark. I don't see a gun. But it still could be there, hidden by the shadows of her body.

I will myself to calm down and think logically.

"You were holding it. And then you looked at me like you were guilty."

"How could you *possibly* tell how I was looking at you? Jesus, Lea."

"What were you doing, then? With the gun?" Then I get it. "You thought *I* might use it."

"I don't know. Maybe. Mostly, I just wanted to be the one who had it, and even when I was holding it, I still didn't feel safe."

Wow.

"We have to get rid of it." I didn't expect to say this, but now that the words have come out of my mouth, I know that it's the right plan. The only plan. "We can't have that gun with us, because neither of us trusts each other with it."

"We can't get rid of it!" Aracely protests. "Someone could use it against us."

"We'll bury it beneath the blood and scatter the bullets. We have to, Aracely. We have to trust each other. I don't think I can survive this without you, but if I'm scared all the time, then I can't survive it *with* you, either."

I sit down in the blood. It soaks through my pants. I don't care.

"I wish I hadn't seen you kill that man. So I wouldn't know what you're capable of."

"I wish I *had* seen you. So I wouldn't have to wonder."

This is horrible. Neither of us should be capable of anything. Neither of us should be wondering anything. We should be debating whether to stay together when I leave for college in the fall. We should be planning our summer. Jumping out onto the big, flat rocks in the river to sunbathe. Betting if this will be the year Hillary's parents finally catch the evil raccoon that lives behind their house and makes a mess of their trash. Aracely and I could take my dad's boat out by the dam and go fishing. We could hike together in the Notch and hold hands, and it wouldn't matter because her friends wouldn't be there to see.

But we can't do any of that. We'll maybe—probably—never get the chance, ever again.

Even if the earth stopped bleeding tomorrow, things wouldn't be fixed. Our planet has betrayed us. It hurt us. It proved that it can do things science can't explain. We can never trust it again. We can never trust each other again.

So many of us destroyed things—destroyed each other—for survival. Everyone I meet for the rest of my life, I will wonder if they had to kill someone. And they'll wonder it about me, too.

We'll have to rebuild everything. Bury all the dead we've left in our homes, in the streets. Regain faith in the world's governments, who couldn't save us from our planet or each other.

I have to trust Aracely. Because I cannot exist in a world where there's no one I trust. But the gun . . .

"It was too easy," I say. "I didn't even mean to do it. I didn't have to think. I had my finger on the trigger so she couldn't put hers there, but somehow I squeezed it and the gun went off and she had a hole in her neck. It probably wouldn't be as easy another time, because now I know exactly what happens. It's not a thing I just imagine anymore, you know? Like, you hear about people shooting each other on the news and you can picture it in your head, and you know it's awful, but you don't *know*. It isn't real until you've fired the gun and you've felt the way it vibrates over and over in your bones like an echo of what you just did. And then you see the person you shot, you see what you did to them, and everything changes. Everything."

Aracely doesn't say anything. She's leaning against a tree. I can't tell through the dark if she's looking at me.

So I go on: "At least, that's how I felt. Maybe murderers with plans don't feel anything. Maybe it's just like they expect. Maybe it all comes together for them. But I never meant to kill anyone. I don't want to be a girl who has killed someone. I want my mom to be alive."

Aracely reaches for my hand, pulling me to my feet. "I don't want to be a girl who has killed someone, either." She touches my face, lightly, with her fingertips. It anchors me in place. "I felt like something dark came out in me when I killed that man. I knew he was probably going to shoot us both no matter what. And he became just this . . . this *thing* to me. Like a spider or a horsefly or something inconsequential except for the fact that he was trying to hurt us. I think it was all adrenaline when I hit him and when I wrapped the twine around his neck, but it got harder after that. He was a person again. His body was shaking under my foot, and he couldn't breathe and it made me feel like *I* couldn't breathe, but I had to keep going because at that point, it was him or us, and I wanted it to be him."

We've done it now: had the conversation we should have had this evening—yesterday evening, really. Every word she said resonates in a deep, damaged part of my heart, and yet I'm not crying. Neither of us are crying. Shouldn't we be crying? I feel like my emotions are a fire that's being smothered by a wet, heavy blanket. They're trying to stay aglow, but the weight of my actions is suffocating them.

"You know we have to get rid of it," I say softly, returning us to the gun. "We're not okay. We can't—"

"I know."

I shiver. The night is cool and my clothing damp.

"Let's do it now," I say.

So we do.

It's Aracely who climbs back up to the loft, while I wait below as an act of trying to rebuild our trust. Clinking noises tell me she's taking out the bullets, and then the rope ladder creaks and she's beside me again.

"Here." She drops the bullets into my hand. Five of them.

I take them outside and I throw them. All in opposite

directions. All but one. One, I shove deep into the dirt with my thumb.

Then I go back into the camp and curl up in the loft, shivering in my bloody clothes. I don't bother trying to wipe any of it off me. I'm past that now. I just have to hope I'll be okay.

Aracely joins me before long. I reach for her hand and curl my fingers around it.

"I'm sorry I ran," I say. "And thank you for not letting me go."

"Just try not to do it again, all right?" She nestles her face into the side of my shoulder.

"I'll try. I promise."

And, finally, I sleep.

32.

This is what Aracely and I have when we set out in the morning:

One lawn mower blade.

One pocketknife.

Two steak knives.

Six nails, pried from the loft.

Two branches we're using as walking sticks.

A chunk of granite, for fire-starting.

A handful of rags and a bundle of twine.

The clothes on our backs.

Each other.

My clothes are stiff and crackly with dried blood. It hurts when my shirt scrapes over the wound on my ribs, and that concerns me a little. I check on it when Aracely's not looking. It looks okay. It's red and a tiny bit swollen, still weeping blood and clear fluid, though that's all probably to be expected when I can't stop it from rubbing on my crusted shirt. There's no point in worrying, I suppose, when there's nothing I can do.

My mouth is as dry as a winter's day. Aracely's lips are cracked, bleeding a little. Her eyes look bruised and sunken.

"We need water," I tell her, my voice a harsh rasp.

"I know. Your dad will have some. Right?"

I nod. He said he did. He'd better.

If he even lets us in.

We trudge out of the trees, back onto the interstate, where the terrain is less unsteady. It's deserted. No one else is foolish enough to try and walk all the way out here from town, it seems. It would have been such a short distance, if we'd managed to drive. Five miles from where we stole the truck to the dam. That's it. Five miles. God, even *walking* shouldn't be taking us this long.

My whole body feels shaky and weak. The sun burns down at me, bright and unrelenting. I cringe away from it, but there's nowhere to go. Out of habit, I sweep my walking stick in front of me to clear the bones out of my path. It snags on hair and unearths a few chunks of broken pavement, but . . . no bones. I think back to last night, to my desperate flight. I remember tripping over a root, but . . .

"Aracely." My voice is a hoarse croak.

She turns her head toward me slowly, her face a mask of exhaustion.

"I think the bones are gone."

Her mouth twists pensively, and then her eyes widen. "You're right. I haven't seen any since . . ."

"Since before the tree."

Could it be true? A tiny spark of hope ignites in my mind, fueling me in place of the food and water that should fill my empty stomach. If the bones are leaving, then maybe . . . maybe the rest will go, too. Maybe this is ending. *Please* let it be ending.

"Come on." Aracely gestures feebly. "We have to . . . keep going."

I nod and force my leaden legs to move forward again. It's hard. A spark of hope is something, but it's not enough. I'm shaky and my stomach keeps cramping with hunger, a hard pain that makes me double over.

"Look," Aracely rasps, pointing with trembling fingers.

We've reached the Connecticut River. We're not close, not yet, but there is the dam, a metal-and-concrete rectangle in the distance. All we have to do is continue following the interstate around the edge of the river, walk down the exit ramp, and we'll be there. We can do this.

Hair coils around my ankle. I can't see it, but I can feel it tightening halfheartedly, like it's making one last attempt.

"Leave me," I tell it, my voice calm and soft.

And . . . it listens. It lets go.

Or maybe it didn't listen, and the timing was just right, because when I feel for it with the toe of my shoe, it's . . . gone.

Aracely doesn't notice any of this; she's already started walking again. We're both more purposeful now, panting like we're mid-marathon but barely sweating at all. My body feels a hundred pounds heavier. I'm hot and cold, and the colors of the world around me have changed, like I'm in that almost hallucinatory state between awake and asleep—or life and death, I suppose.

I'm so dehydrated. Dangerously dehydrated.

I fall to my knees. I cannot support my own weight anymore.

"Lea?" Aracely wavers in front of me.

"I . . . can't. I'll crawl."

It isn't long before Aracely falls, too. We crawl-slither inch-by-inch along the road, so slowly. My hands and knees ache from knocking against rock and broken pavement, rougher-edged now that the cushion of hair is diminishing. Everything hurts so much, but I have to keep going, *have to*.

"We aren't going to make it today," I say to Aracely. It

hurts to speak. The words scrape against my sandpaper throat. "The sun . . ."

The sun is setting, is what I want to tell her, but I'm too tired to finish.

"We need water. We had that jerky and we haven't . . . the heat and the walking and . . . we need water."

We didn't plan this well at all. That's what neither of us says. We didn't count on the earth working so hard against us. We counted on making it to the dam two days ago and not having to worry about food or water or anything.

We are idiots.

Idiots who are next to a river. A swollen river whose gentle waves lap at the edge of the guardrails lining the interstate. I saw something a while ago about what to do if you need to drink contaminated water. Boil it. Distill it. We could . . .

But we don't have fire or matches or wood.

Plenty of trees nearby. But could we . . . ?

"Could we make fire?" I ask. "If we drink something, we could keep walking and then . . ."

And then we would make it there tonight. To safety.

"Granite, pocketknife," Aracely says.

A cluster of tangled driftwood poking up out of the murk becomes our firewood. Aracely slams the chunk of granite against my pocketknife until the little slivers of metal become sparks and then, finally, a tiny fire.

She coaxes our tenuous baby fire into something bigger, hotter, while I scavenge a couple broken beer bottles from the road's edge. I dip them carefully into the water, hopefully skimming off a top layer that's more water than blood.

We won't be able to distill it, not with what resources or skills we have available, but hopefully boiling will be enough. We shouldn't be drinking it at all, but at this point, drinking it is the lesser of two evils. If we don't, we'll succumb to a different kind of insanity.

And we'll probably die.

Besides, if the bones and the hair have gone away, and the blood levels have lowered to only a few inches, then maybe the water is in better condition than it was. We have to hope.

I edge the bottles carefully next to the fire, hoping it's true what I saw on TV once, that you can actually boil water in something like this without melting or shattering it.

This better work.

This *has* to work.

It seems like a lifetime before the water starts to bubble.

"How long?" Aracely croaks.

I shrug. "Little longer."

After the water has boiled for what seems like long enough, I grab the bottles one at a time with a shirt sleeve pulled over my hand, and move them to where they're mostly but not completely submerged in the bloody river water, hoping this'll cool them faster. As soon as the bottles are cool enough to touch with our bare hands without burning us, we drink. We do it simultaneously, dumping the water into our open mouths, over our faces.

It tastes like hot copper, sick and sour. Still, it wets my throat, makes my swollen tongue sigh with relief, moisturizes my painful, cracked lips.

But my stomach rejects it almost immediately. With a twist in my gut, I fall to my knees and vomit wretchedly onto the ground. My body heaves and heaves until my ribs feel cracked and my lungs can't catch enough breath.

I'm vaguely aware that Aracely is beside me, doing the same.

"Fuck it," I say. My voice sounds now like a person who's smoked their lungs into oblivion. "I'm walking."

My vision skips, clicks from object to object like I'm playing a game on a computer with a shitty graphics card. I climb-stumble over the guardrails, back onto the interstate. And then I'm confused.

Which way am I going?

Where's Aracely?

Why is the moon so pretty?

I start to cry, because the moon is so beautiful my heart can't take it.

We aren't going to make it to the dam. We weren't meant to, I don't think. When everyone's dying around you, sometimes it's best that you don't survive, either. What painful memories to be left with.

This is for the best.

This is what the blood wanted. This is why it called to me when I was in my house. It knew my fate. Knew what I would do and knew that I would need to die, in the end. The blood wanted to make it a beautiful death, a death to be remembered.

I laugh through my sobs.

I've entirely lost what threads of my sanity remained. They snapped somewhere between the river and here. Or maybe the bile that charred my throat burned right through my mind, too.

But I'm *aware* of the loss, and that's something. That's how I know what's happening now is right. That's how I know it's going to be okay.

I lay down in the blood. It isn't deep at all anymore, and it feels kind of nice. I'm surrounded by a warm blanket of liquid. I was right before; the blood is beautiful. God-sent. It's meant to make everything better, and it's our own fault that things have gotten worse.

The blood isn't trying to hurt me. It's protecting me. Keeping me warm while I wait.

Wait for death to take me.

33.

I'm cold.

Sun shines blindingly down onto my face, but I'm cold.

It's hard to open my eyes. They're so dry. Everything's so dry and painful and bright.

I spread my fingers slowly apart. They peel stickily from each other, encrusted with something. I hold one hand in front of my face, squinting against the sun's harsh blaze. Dried blood. Dried . . . but aren't I lying on the ground?

I sit up quickly. Everything rotates around me and I clutch at the earth for support. I'm touching the ground. Dry ground. The blood is gone, *gone*!

"Aracely!" I shout. Except my throat is so dry, it comes out barely a whisper.

Where is she? I stumble to my feet and have to stay completely still for several long moments before my vision stops spinning around me. My stomach spasms weakly, but there's nothing in it. I'm dry as a bone, empty as this road. I don't think my body has the energy to throw up anyway, even if it wanted to. My feet hurt, and I realize I have no idea where my shoes are.

There.

Unmoving, a few feet away from me, is a still, dark-haired form.

My overworked heart pounds even harder. "Aracely," I rasp again, shambling toward her.

She is breathing. Oh, thank God, she's breathing.

I poke at her with my foot, and she moans and opens her eyes.

"Am I dead?" she asks, her voice just as crackly and faint as mine. "It's so bright."

"It's gone," I whisper. "The blood is gone. The bones, the hair, all of it's gone."

She sits up, shading her eyes with a trembling hand. "So we *are* dead, then."

"We're not. We can't be. If we were dead, we wouldn't feel like this."

She looks around, confused. "Then . . . then we better get to your dad."

I help her up, nearly toppling myself back to the ground in the process. I'm so dry and hot and disoriented. Every time I take a step, I have to pause and wait for the world to stop spinning. We made it farther during our hallucinatory wanderings last night than I would have expected; we're already midway down the off-ramp. We're so *close*.

The ground is rust-red with dried blood. The pavement cracked and warped. Wisps of hair flutter in the branches of a nearby tree, and a small heap of bones sits just off the edge of the road. Maybe remnants from the disaster, maybe the fleshless remains of someone recently deceased.

I don't ponder it too hard.

Nothing tries to hurt us as we limp down the off-ramp and across the adjacent road. Nothing whispers lies about the sweetness of death into our brains. I don't trust the silence, the peace. Maybe it makes sense that the blood would leave as abruptly and inexplicably as it arrived. But I want more closure. I want to know why it's gone. If it's truly gone. How am I supposed to reconcile all that's happened to me if I don't understand?

"We made it," Aracely whispers when we step onto the crisp brown grass of the lawn that edges the dam.

"We did."

A bird sits on one of the posts near the dam. An actual living bird. Something grayish brownish white—a mourning dove, maybe? It tilts its head to the side, like it's startled to see us, and then takes flight.

The bird triggers a lightness in my heart: a hope. It takes me by surprise. I didn't know I was still capable of hope. I like the feeling, and I nurture it in my chest. The world has changed, irreversibly, no matter what happens now. But maybe some things can be like they were. Our memories will be tainted with darkness, but our futures can be filled with light. That's the thought I hold on to as Aracely and I shuffle clumsily across the lawn.

A few steps from the concrete bridge of the dam, my foot squelches in damp ground.

We're near the river. I'm not going to look down, because there'll be nothing to see. It's just water.

Aracely stops. I reach for her hand. This is not the time to hesitate, to question, to look at the ground beneath our feet. We're both so thirsty and so tired. We shouldn't trust ourselves.

Hand in hand, Aracely and I walk out onto the cement structure of the dam. It burns my feet, but that's okay because we're almost there. It feels far, but it isn't. I see the door, shimmering like a mirage. If I didn't know it was real, I might despair. But I've been here millions of times. We just have to make it across this walkway and we will be safe and watered and fed.

The fear that my dad might not want me anymore is gone. He's too good of a man to send his daughter away in this condition. I'll tell him everything, and we'll get past it all.

Pink-tinged water surrounds us, much clearer than it was yesterday. The remnants of the blood are draining, and hopefully the toxins with it. This is the start of the world's new beginning, of life after blood.

On the right is the front of the dam. Here the water barely stirs. The sun reflects off its glassy surface in a stripe of light.

And on our left, the water crashes in waves down the back of the dam. A swirling, roaring froth of liquid fury battling trees and grasses and itself for space.

Right: peace. Left: chaos. Straight ahead: sanctuary.

Droplets of water from the roaring spray hit my skin. The liquid looks pinker close up. But it's clearing itself out. I know it is.

I'm weeping by the time we drag ourselves to the door. My eyes are too dry for tears and my throat too dry for noise, but there's a catch in my lungs and a hurt in my chest that let me know I'm crying.

We both raise trembling fists to the door. Our knocking is weak, but the sound reverberates through the metal.

It takes a few minutes, but finally, with a grating noise, the door opens. I fall to my knees. Dad stands before me, haloed by the sunlight. It takes me three tries to rasp out, "Dad."

He just stands there for a moment, such a long moment, and I'm scared I won't pass his judgment, scared he'll turn me away. Then he kneels in front of me and I see that his face is slick with tears. He hugs me tightly.

"You made it," he says.

"But I . . . with Mom . . . you thought . . ."

"Shhh." He kisses my hair. "We don't have to talk about that now. We'll get you two some water and something to eat, and then we'll figure out what to do about the rest, okay?"

He pulls me gently to my feet. I lean heavily on him, because now that I've fallen, I don't know how I was supporting my weight in the first place. Dad notices Aracely then, beside me.

"Aracely," he says gently. "I'm so glad to meet you."

He takes her arm, too, and smiles, and leads us both inside.

It's darker in here, darker and cool. It smells of damp cement and vibrates with the hum of machinery from all the mechanisms working below our feet. Finally, I feel calm. Dad's arm is secure around me, an unspoken promise not to give up on me, not to abandon me despite what I did.

Someone shoves a cup of water into my hands, and I drink it shakily, spilling it all down myself. It's cool and refreshing; it's *life*.

The world might be mending or it might not. Right now, that's not important.

What's important is that Aracely and I, we made it. We survived.

We are safe.

Acknowledgements:

I may have been the one to write this book, but there are so many people who have helped me along the way. I could write another entire novel to express my gratitude, but I will try to keep it brief:

My agent, Sarah LaPolla, who sold this book *twice*. You never gave up on me or on *Bleeding Earth*. You are the best advocate I could possibly ask for. If I could take my appreciation for you and turn it into a physical object, it would be bigger than the solar system.

My editor, Jordan Hamessley, who *bought* this book twice. I am so lucky to have an editor who truly understands and loves this novel, and who has worked so hard to help me make it the best it can be. You made the bloodpocalypse come to life.

Everyone at Adaptive Books. Thank you so much for taking a chance on a debut author and her bloody book.

Kate Hart, Kirsten Hubbard, and Michelle Schusterman. Without the three of you, this book literally would not exist. Thank you for the ridiculous amount of support and enthusiasm you gave when I told you I had this idea. For that and so much more, I am grateful beyond words.

Amy Lukavics. You are a glorious human and I'm not sure what I'd do if I didn't have you to love horror and *Tomb Raider* with me.

The ladies at YA Highway (past and present!) I admire you all so much, and am fortunate to have your friendship, commiseration, and moose jokes.

My coworkers. You all have been so great, and I'm thankful for how supportive you've been through the ups and downs of my journey to publication.

My parents, Denis and Jeanne Ward. You were my first supporters and you are my best supporters. I am the luckiest person in the world to have been born to the best parents in the world.

Jackie Ward. You are the best sister. Thank you for thinking I was someone worth looking up to (at least sometimes) when we were kids. I think you're worth looking up to, too.

Andrea Millett and Elaine Millett. When you marry someone, you marry their family, and I got pretty lucky.

Brandon Millett. I know you don't always understand this whole book writing thing, but thank you for supporting it anyway. I'm so glad I get to go through this life with you. I love you.

Michael. My favorite human. You are the most wonderful, lively, hilarious child and you make my life complete.

And last but not least: you, the person holding this book right now. This is all for you. Thank you for reading, and I hope you enjoy!